ADVENTURES

WITH THE

ANGELS OF LOVE

Marlena

ADVENTURES

WITH THE

ANGELS OF LOVE

By
Marlena Tanya Muchnick

ISBN: 1-58721-991-3

Marlena Tanya Muchnick
myambra@hotmail.com
http://jewishconvert-lds.com
Please also access the website for updates on forthcoming books,
events and miscellany.

Available in ebook and softcover

Cover and all illustrations by Denise A. Parrish
Seattle, Washington

Manufactured in the United States of America

1stBooks – rev. 01/12/01

Other books by the author

Notes of a Jewish Convert to the LDS Church:
Conversion of a Soul
(also as an ebook)

Life Changing Testimonies of the Lord Jesus Christ

Available as an ebook under the title:
Powerful Testimonies of Jesus Christ

Acknowledgement

I am grateful to three sweet sisters who helped me with this book. In particular, Glenda Perryman, whose idea it was. Natalie Bumgardner, illustrator Denise Parrish, Bill and Dori Davis offered incisive criticism and saw possibilities beyond my limited view. My thanks also to Donna Prisbrey, for her editorial comments. As for the helpers who cannot be seen with our jaded eyes, this adventure is their reward.

Dedication

For the bright lights in *my* firmament

Mahana Lesieli, Margaret Ann,
Martin Morris, Markie,
and Meredith Rose

Epiphany

Awakened from the clockwork world
Angels beckoned me
To richer lands suffused with life,
Radiant with love.

The sound of choirs was a hymn to God.

It became my voice.
In silence I sang.
First in worldly age, then in youth,
Until merely the child[1] beheld
His unblemished Light.

Amazed, I entered in
And found my place.
It was then I learned what is real.

[1] Mark 10:15, 3Ne 9:22

Each life becomes a testament
to what its spirit has determined
is true.

Part One: Finding the Wind

One

Brigham Young, the second and sometimes the most controversial Mormon prophet, used to give sermons on the ways in which God spoke to His mortals on earth. Brother Brigham said that revelation is the Lord's mind and will. It lets us know what God desires of us, *so that we will do it.* To those who complain that God no longer reveals anything to humans but hardness, toil and tougher times, President Young scoffed "I could give you revelation as fast as a man could run." He added that indeed he was at that moment receiving divine instruction and, with his marvelous manner of saying exactly the pithy thing, he added

"Do you want more revelation written? Wait until you obey what is already written."

The man who spoke those words at sacrament meeting was fresh from the holy wars of missionary work, come home to his ward in their small town in the Pacific Northwest. They hit young Ruthann Mirra with prophetic power. His own emotions found hers and lifted her heart. That was not long after her mother filed for divorce and her father had to move out of the house to keep the peace. Ruth's parents had problems that caused them to disagree often, but that last day their final scene together all but broke her heart. Ruth was eleven when it happened. Children, because they are intuitive, also hurt from the pain their parents suffer. Ruth cherished her father's presence in their home and when he left them she became a solitary child almost at once, prone to wandering in the garden or reading love stories and poetry to quiet her troubled spirit.

After school, she let the library claim her attention. While her mother was away at work Ruth made friends with the many characters she found in the books. They were her only society outside the Church. Because of her quiet ways and plain features she was not sought out by her schoolmates. When eventually the boys and girls in her classes discovered their natural desires for one another, Ruth was apart, she began developing instead small talents within herself, learning to garden, to enjoy music, to draw. She spent many hours writing her impressions of these things in an environment of self-discovery, though she learned of life mostly from books and other works filled with the reflections of other minds. After her graduation she spoke of attending the college in the valley an hour's drive from home. Her mother was happy about Ruth's plans and together they spoke excitedly of her future success as a woman "of substance". Her mother counseled her and told her that Heavenly Father had something very special for her.

A picture of Jesus Christ hung on the wall of Ruth's bedroom. She had put it there the week her father and mother had that final argument. It soothed her spirit. Every time Ruth walked into her room she knew the eyes of the Savior were upon her. While she was young her prayers came effortlessly morning and night. She delighted in speaking with her Heavenly Father. Listening on her knees after prayer she sometimes heard the Spirit whisper to her mind that she was God's most special prize, and she would shudder involuntarily with excitement. Sometimes she took the picture off the wall and stared at it. "I feel I can read his mind," she would tell her mother. In church, tears would come so unexpectedly. Her ward leaders were quick to notice Ruth's spirituality. They guided her toward a life of study and application. Ruth's bishop, a gentle servant, counseled

4

her to study the prophets whose teachings contained the jewels of life and salvation.

She did this for a while, but her passion for the Gospel was often in competition with her desire for a life in the world. In her mother's antique full-length mirror the daughter visualized a prominent writer, a traveler, a woman of noble spirituality and accomplishment. She felt that a golden opportunity would come her way, meant for her only because she had been "chosen" for something special and different. Somewhere a soul was waiting to speak out, precious moments had been lived and needed the telling. Ruth would come nobly to the rescue and thereby assure her own fame as well. For a long time these dreams were her only solace, and they became as prophecy to her.

After college Ruth found steady work as a substitute teacher of English to middle school students, a job she took only for quick experience and a living wage. She promised herself that in a few years opportunity would find her returning to a university working on more meaningful projects in preparation for her shining future. But the job became a challenge as she was asked to take on extra work. The years filed by and graduate school still waited. Students liked her but they were slow to grasp the rudiments of English and she felt it was because of her lack as a teacher. Eventually she grew angry with her classes because she believed they were at fault. Then the school grew larger. Ruth was given more classes and an administrative position, which she tolerated. After a while she found that she depended upon the security of that dulling routine, though her attention wandered often while she was teaching.

"I'm afraid I'm settling in," she said to her mother. "Next year I'll ask for a leave and go to the university."

But when her mother became ill and needed supervision, Ruth put her ambition on hold another year. Her mother's illness took her savings for university tuition. One more year, she thought. Have to be patient. But the ruts of her life deepened. Her mother's care ate away at her spare time. Slowly the deep frustration in the sameness of her routine and her own lack of confidence dampened her faith in any future beyond the classroom. In frustration one day she threw out the university catalog and turned her mother's mirror to the wall.

———————————

Despite her preoccupations, opportunity came. It happened in an odd way, between a departing harsh winter cold and spring's sprouting allergies. Ruth was trapped amidst four classes of term papers propped on bottles of cold remedy. The missionaries had just given her a blessing and hurriedly gone. There was a small knock at the door. After a short wait the knock came again.. Groaning and reluctant Ruth arose and trudged through the room. Rarely did anyone come to call at such a time without an invitation.

Dripping in the doorway stood a child about six, wrapped in her best coat, rain hat upon dark locks. It was a little sister of a student. Wet from a sudden spring shower, she held a bag in her tiny hands.

"Come in, dear. Claudia, is it? Take off that wet coat and hat."

The child was too cold to smile, but she came in quickly and shut the door, dropping her bag on the carpet. Two towels and a glass of warm milk later she remembered her mission.

"Mommy wants you to have this," she said, offering the plastic bag up to Ruth. It contained only a smaller sack of cookies.

"Mommy is sick, too, but she said you should call my very great grandfather."

Claudia used her chubby hands for emphasis, spreading them out further and bobbing her head at *great*.

"He's visiting us for a little while and Mommy says he wants to tell you his story." She eyed the cookies.

"His story? I don't know your 'very great grandfather,' sweetie. Are you sure?"

Ruth wondered why Claudia's mother hadn't called with the request, but perhaps she felt just as ill and didn't want to cough her way through a conversation.

6

"All I know is Mommy says you have to call him. Mommy says that this grandpa needs to tell it because he is sick and he wants to leave something for his family before he goes to Heavenly Father."

With that said in her matter-of-fact voice Claudia continued to look at the cookies until Ruth obliged her with one. She wondered why the child's mother would choose a seldom-published, overwrought English teacher to record her grandfather's story. Ruth was not friends with the woman and had been rather stern with her son, David, whose progress in composition would never be rewarded with more than passing grades. Questioning Claudia further, Ruth learned that her great grandfather was quite ill and very fragile of age. This request was evidently one of his dying wishes and there was no time to be lost. Ruth was the only writer they knew.

The logic of the cryptic message was hard to deny. The assignment did sound interesting. As Ruth sent the child home she remembered that children were natural carriers of simple truths that would be overlooked without their innocent observations. She remembered the Christ child. He sent beautiful messages of peace to all the world even before he spoke. Perhaps angels sometimes send children to us in their own place as messengers, that in their sweet innocence some most valiant work can be accomplished.

After Claudia left, Ruth reached inside the bag to find a cookie but her hand pulled out a piece of paper. She had forgotten to obtain the phone number to call and was just about to run after Claudia when she saw that the paper contained the number needed, with the words "Hurry. Much to tell. Little time left." It was unsigned.

The phone call did not yield much. Ruth spoke with a woman who advised her of the route to the aged man's home and gave a time of arrival. Marshall Cannon, a widower, lived miles north in a small coastal town along the Puget Sound waterways. It sounded like a dull and difficult ride and Ruth wanted to call back and break the appointment, despite Claudia's urgent message, but she'd misplaced the phone number amid the term papers and by the time she found it, she decided to take the offer.

Ruth was directed to an avenue near an old warehouse. Her path had been carefully described. She wrote it in detail, then committed it to memory. Something told her she would make this trip more than once. The drive was a long one. She felt foolish. I haven't even been asked to agree to see him, she argued with herself. A *child* told me that I must. Yet she felt almost responsible for helping, as though it was some work of charity that must be done and Ruthann Mirra had been impressed (conned was the better word) to comply. She was not sure what urged her on, other than a curiosity to know what this man had to say. She assumed he was LDS because David's family were Church members. She reasoned that there might also be genuine historical value in his remembrances. And surely his years had brought him wisdom. How could anyone know the trials they would face in mortality? Perhaps in his long years on earth this old man had wonderful stories to tell that Ruth could draw on for her own work. She would be diligent. Treat it like an excursion, an outing along the Sound that would afford her time to plan tomorrow's lesson.

The path to Marshall Cannon's home was steep and long, protected by cedars that made a bower. It was completely hidden from the main road. Ruth was grateful for good directions. Finding through the trees a small clearing and an even smaller cottage, she pulled her little car into the driveway. Before her a large and carefully tended garden spanned the length of the front yard. It boasted red and yellow nasturtiums in cascade over a fence that upheld and encouraged them, like tender arms that kept its myriad babies safe from the whims of strangers who might stray here to pick their lovely and scattered variety.

Ruth walked along the flowered path to the entrance and knocked, an echo of the knock that had sent her there, and stepped back while the weathered wooden door opened and she was ushered inside.

8

The entryway was full of light that streamed in from the large windows across from the entryway, revealing a long, low-ceilinged room bordered by an outside deck that held ivy and bougainvilla. The bay was below in the distance, shimmering in the coming sunset. The smell of fresh bread hung in the air from the general direction of the small kitchen off the main hall. Ruth felt an instant hunger, though she had eaten before leaving on her trip. Her welcomer, a short, very round woman of advanced age greeted her with a quick smile, then turned and led her through the cluttered living room to a smaller one that smelled wonderfully of leather and a waft of apple blossom. Ruth recognized her voice from their phone conversation earlier that week.

"Wait here, now, and he'll be out soon," the woman sweetly commanded her and left to get him. Nervously, Ruth settled into an adjacent chair to await her host. It was a place of repose, informal and quietly comfortable. A sweet spirit lingered. Ruth sensed a new anticipation, as if her life was being placed now in the hands of someone who had not yet appeared. It was very disconcerting. She stood again, pacing the room impatiently.

The sound of footsteps in the carpeted hallway. They were slow and determined, as if each foot was deliberately picked up and set down in unsteady haste. Another, a tapping sound, punctuated the unsteady intervals coming from the cocoon of the hall passageway.

Two

Marshall Cannon came into the room with swagger, a seaman's roll, like he had waited his life to find her and the air came suddenly alive with his entrance. His brown cane thrust at the woman in greeting. She was surrounded by his energy. It shocked her. The man stared at her an instant, then put his head back and laughed with enthusiasm. Brown eyes jolly and dancing in his creased old face smiled down at her. He wore heavy clothing from hunting in the forested acreage behind his home. His white hair was still thick as froth in places and the beard that tumbled across his collar curled about his chin like a whitecap. His grin revealed a dented silver-capped molar. When he offered his large hand down to her she realized that he was well over six feet. Then he just stood there, energetic, vibrant, smelling of the chilly air, a vivacious spirit in a body weighted with time.

Something's wrong, she thought at first sight of him. She had expected him to be weak. She'd been told he was sick. But his eyes were alive with interest as he smiled at her. She let him lead her to an old leather chair and hold her hand while she seated herself.

Soundlessly, he made a little bow to her. Though he had unusual height he was not stooped. He tingled with nervous energy and she felt pulled toward him. A long, sensitive nose was his prominent feature, thick white brows were flags across his eyes. His cheekbones, weathered like his hands, were scarred white. His extreme age he bore unaware, as if time had reluctantly hidden its destruction in his bones but could or would not invade his cheerful countenance.

"I trust you found this old place all right? When I built this house I tried to hide it from near everyone so I could work unbothered."

He guffawed as he moved to his leather chair, gesticulating with his cane. Ruth had never seen one like it, sleek and lacquered. A small, worn, but finely carved figure of a smiling cherub rose out from the curve just below his grip.

11

"I'm Marshall Cannon, the oldest man in town. You are…?"

The woman was hesitant. She introduced herself as his great nephew's English teacher, sent by his daughter to act as a recorder of genealogical information. He must have known that, she thought. Was he teasing or had he already forgotten that she had come at his request? He stared vacantly at her for a few seconds and then laughed and slapped his good right leg.

"Oh, yes, yes. You're Miss Mirra, my David's English teacher, the one who keeps him after school a lot. Yes, good job. That boy needs lots of discipline or he won't pay attention to his studies. Glad you're keeping an eye on that boy. He'll turn out well if he's kept to the task, to the wheel. Yep, I'd like to be around when he's a man, to give him my boat, but time grows short for me, I guess you can tell."

He looked at her and knew she was the one. How many times had he prayed aloud that he be given this favor, this last chance? She was not past thirty, slender, plain and neat. He sensed her sweet spirit. Her hair touched her nape and was neatly rolled into a bun there. She looked professional to him, like someone who would teach his grandson English. Her eyes were alert and she was taking in everything.

"Enough about David. Let's talk about you. My granddaughter tells me you're also a writer? That true? You a good one?"

He leaned forward and peered at her, trying to see behind her self-containment. She didn't look like any writer. Too reserved and shy. She was a hard one to read, all right. He tapped an emphasis with his cane.

His questioning made her a little uncomfortable. Even the idea that he could ask if she were a good writer she thought rude. Claudia's mother had thought so. Claudia had said her great grandfather was dying, so Ruth expected to find a bedridden patient, eager for her help in recording his last words and thankful for her timely appearance at his bedside. She'd brought her tape recorder and pad, even a mike to record the last words. But the man before her was someone else. This man was full of vitality. Why, he could take the recorder and tape himself. Ruth sighed. She would go on home and finish those essays that needed grading before the week was over.

"You a good writer? I didn't hear your answer."

He turned up his hearing aids until she could hear them whistle. She smiled tightly and looked past him through the window of his study. Marshall Cannon looked at her. He sensed her hesitation and it worried him.

"I have sold a few articles. I'm mainly a teacher, though. I instruct high school youth in the proper use of the English language and I write as an avocation. Mostly fiction."

She mentioned the note she'd received which bade her come in response to his urgent request for someone to record his memoirs. Marshall was silent a moment, then reached for the glass of water at his side. Her formality with him he interpreted as fear. She had come, that was enough. He would convince her to stay.

"Yes, my memoirs. I have a story to tell, and it's a true one. Kept it a secret all these years... Only one person's heard it. My family, I don't know what they'll think of it. I'm an old man, you can see that. I'm going home to the Lord soon enough, that's why it's so important. The time has come. I really hope you'll help me, make notes, organize the tapes and oversee the whole thing. I want you to put it all together. A month or two. That may be all the time I have left. I'll pay you well, oh, yes, don't you worry about that."

He saw that she was considering his words, but he couldn't guess what she was thinking.

Marshall fumbled for a handkerchief from his back pocket and blew his nose loudly. Ruth was looking at him, then at her hands, trying to decide. He wondered what was holding her back. Maybe she needed to be prompted.

"How soon can you start?"

Ruth felt silly for hesitating. There was no time to think this out. She had just met this man but he seemed so eager for her help. She didn't want the assignment, didn't want to feel that she had to be counted on in this way. Things were set, the way they'd been for years, routine, wrapped in the certainty of knowing what was coming each day and night. This trip was a mistake, she could see now that it would hold no discoveries. It was secretarial work, charity work, but how could she get out of it? After all, David was her student, and David's mother was a member of her stake. She felt touched that the old man wanted her to stay.

"Did you want someone to begin right away? I... well, I could start soon, Mr. Cannon. To take dictation and organize the material. I will... do what I can," she said. You say there's just one story?"

Marshall breathed with relief. He stood up and jammed his cane against the floor resolutely and his high spirit returned.

"Just one, but it's a long one. Well, fine. Good decision. We can start work today. Glad to have you aboard, my dear. What did you say your name is?"

She tried to return his smile.

"Ruthann is my name," she said, rising from her seat. "But everyone calls me Ruth."

Marshall came around the table and put out his hand, creased and dry like old wood, to seal the agreement.

"Ruth, then. You just follow me now to the study. Be more comfortable there, and Mrs. Willow will bring us lunch."

He led the way determinedly back down the musty old hallway to his office, leaning his right leg against the cane. At times like this he hated being a cripple. It didn't help to think of the years when his body was sound as a bullet, when he ran along the bay shore or sailed his own ship across the Sound alone in winds that threatened to send him overboard. His life had been a busy enterprise, filled with adventure. His cane tapped out the steps to his study. Suddenly the searing memory of that day when he battled for Naida's life and his own came at him, as it had almost daily for many years. It had happened so quickly, a life come to take life away. He saw her vividly, her face contorted, her lovely hair covered with her blood. How long now, sixty years ago? A lifetime, maybe two had passed. I will be with you soon, my lovely one, his heart said to his picture of her. He moaned to himself and pushed the thoughts away.

The sound of classical violins met their ears. Marshall began to hum with it absently, his heart lightening with the sound. This

14

story he had to tell was to be his last "voyage". He had planned it that way. For the woman who walked just behind, it would become a path of adventure that led to country strange but not new, real and unimagined.

Three

Marshall's office was a study in excess. It was the only room in the house that overflowed with books and manuals, pictures and memorabilia. The books were everywhere, stacked on chairs and in large wooden bookcases alongside the spacious walls of the room. In the middle sat his oversized mahogany desk, also piled with papers and volumes of nautical information. Ruth recognized many books on Church history. There were tomes on shipping, navigation, tonnage and salvage. Boxes on the floor contained what appeared to be engine parts. Upon questioning Marshall, Ruth learned it was once a working sextant, used in navigation. Marshall had been a navigational engineer along the northern waterways.

"I didn't retire until they took their ship away from me," he told her without humor. Just behind the desk were homemade shelves filled with spiritual videos and tapes. A large picture showing Jesus holding a child upon his lap hung on that wall above the bookcases. Another of him speaking to a rich man was across the room, near the entrance. From where the old sailor sat this picture was always before him.

A busy room might represent a busy mind, but order in all things is a useful habit in a teacher's life, Ruth believed. As Marshall moved around his office she saw herself tidying it up, putting away his files, substituting bookmarks for the folded-down page tops of the journals, stacking and filing the messy papers. She would never be able to work in such chaos and she regretted this situation more by the minute.

Marshall tapped around to his desk and settled gratefully into the large leather chair behind it while Ruth took a dusty armchair near him. He liked her being there, he hoped she would loosen her reserve so he could speak freely to her, like a captain to his first mate. His own fear that she would not take the job was largely gone for the time being, so his mind raced ahead to the start of their work together while he watched her. She seemed fascinated by the objects before her.

A gold plated ship's register with a wide, gold bezel lay on the desktop. Constructed very much like a large watch, it housed three black dials, each accompanied by sets of numbers within a circle representing a scale of nautical miles. Further down the desk a carved brown bear in attack mode lunged toward her, a discordant note. It shared space beside a delicate wooden model of a single-masted sailing boat of singular beauty. Constructed of black mahogany, its sails were starched white cotton. It teetered on the edge of the desk amid the confusion of papers. The room looked to her like a grown man's playground. Leaning precipitously off a shelf behind the desk a framed picture of a young woman smiled. Ruth noted her high cheekbones and soft dark eyes. She looked Asian. Who was she?

Following their lunch Marshall Cannon talked about his numerous family and interviewed Ruth with interest about her own background. Marshall estimated he would only need her services for two months, filled with many meetings and clarification of details. He asked her to tape record his conversation with her microphone. She must then clean up his grammar and smooth over the rough spots, typing it finally for binding in family journals that would be distributed according to his granddaughter's instruction, as she was the commissioning agent in this matter. To this Ruth agreed. It was a neat and accurate way of recording unique oral history. She could see the task would not be difficult. She determined to keep a small personal journal of their time together, documenting their meetings and her impressions. Those she would not turn over to the family. She was to receive a sum of money commensurate to the task and permission to use anecdotes from his story, with proper care for her subject's privacy, of course. And so the deal was struck.

Notes: August 1:

"Begin with these words:"

"Dear Precious Ones, God works miracles with His children, when they allow it. I know, because I was a rough, unruly boy and were it not for His merciful intervention I'd have brought myself and my family to ruin, sending my eternal promise to Davy Jones' Locker. As God is the miracle Worker, we are His miracle keepers!"

"I am an only child. I always wanted brothers and sisters, but all my good folks got was me and all I got was them! They expected me to spend a lot of time in their sights. But I was a traveler and a brawler. There were so many things for a boy to explore back then: a new city, streets and alleyways full of opportunities to grab and run! I ran with some tough fellers. We formed a gang, the Gulf Boys. We found all kinds of things there, scrap metal to be sold, soda and beer bottles to claim deposits on, coins found that had fallen out of the pockets of other little thieves. Many's the milk bottles we swiped off front porches and sold to grocery stores for movie and candy money. Sometimes we stole things and then sold the goods or traded for other things, like tobacco and cheap wine. We pretended to be pirates."

"Now in those days, homelessness was a big problem. Immigration created murderous competition for jobs. My family was poor. I felt it was my duty to help out, but I did it in the wrong way. Sometimes I brought home the things I stole, but my folks were good people, trying to set a good example for me, so they always refused to take anything. All they did was to reprimand me for stealing. I listened, but I wouldn't take their advice. Hey, I didn't care what anyone thought. I was no more than a petty thief."

There was remorse in his voice, his eyes searched a scene long past. But Marshall was also being careful to build the story for his posterity to understand the events that were to follow. This was not to be merely a reminiscence but a lesson in faith and perseverance. Ruth took notes as he spoke. He reached for his well-used Book of Mormon.

19

"Here it is, 1Nephi 12:17, where the angel of the Lord speaks to Nephi about the 'mists of darkness.'"

And the mists of darkness are the temptations of the devil, which blindeth the eyes, and hardeneth the hearts of the children of men, and leadeth them away into broad roads, that they perish and are lost.

"My parents and church leaders tried to teach me these things, but I wouldn't listen to them. I was caught up in the things of the world and I walked the broad roads. I thought that if I wanted something it was right for me to possess it. The world seemed bright but my spirit lived in darkness. I wasn't even twelve, not dry behind the ears, but my path of rebellion was becoming set. A kid like me could go on forever. I wanted all the world had to offer and I never thought about the effects all that running around would have."

Marshall sighed. He rose and moved around his study, picking up the rusty compass on his desk and turned it over, feeling its cool metal. He was a young boy again, adrift in the Sound, oars gone, the rain beating him, praying for his life while he clutched that same tool. I'm so scared, that little boy cried out. I don't want to die! So many years ago, forever. It was all so fresh again that he could smell the rain on his shirt.

Ruth watched the old man move around. As he reached for his compass she saw his eyes water, unaware of her. Why does wisdom come so late, she wondered to herself. When we are young we live in the moment. Do we have to get old before our lives take on meaning?

Marshall wiped his eyes on his shirt and smiled sheepishly.

"Get a little teary now and again. Can't be helped. Back then one of my favorite things was to steal from the outdoor markets in the city's food district. Tables full of food and cheap jewelry, leather caps and jackets, lots of interesting stuff to a boy. I'd grab some fruit and run off, not really because of hunger but just for the thrill it gave me to steal and risk getting caught. I stole things my mother probably didn't even know existed. I rode those old streetcars with their screeching steel wheels. Today they'd be like caterpillars moving up and down the street! Didn't want anyone to know I was just a poor kid from a nearby small town."

Ruth checked the tape recorder to be sure it was picking up the sound properly.

"Why were you so wild? Didn't your parents have control over you?"

"My father did what he could to stop me. He knew, I think, that in my childish mind anything that fanned a passion or filled my belly was justified. That was the only truth I wanted to understand. Rebellion became my banner. No one could stop me. I was headed for real trouble later on."

Marshall talked about his enduring love for the sea and the waterfront where he grew up. He remembered clearly the coolness of the sand after the tide washed out, swimming out to sea until he disappeared in the waves.

"My friends were sure I'd drowned. One time I climbed out on a narrow wooden bridge, but I tripped and almost fell in the water. I clung there to a beam for hours before someone came and rescued me. That day I hurt my dignity quite a bit! Have an old picture of myself back then, just a wiry young fellow with messy hair and a ratty old cap I won in a back lot craps game."

He laughed aloud. " I loved life, Ruth. Just went out and grabbed it!"

Ruth thought of her own childhood, safe and filled with common things. Secretly she'd wished to travel the big cities, to see exhibits of fine art, to hear symphonies play in concert halls. But her father had worked in the nearby city, commuting each day. They could afford few outings away from their home base. Her mom was content to be at home, so Ruth had never traveled beyond the limits of her home state until she was grown.

"Were your parents members of the Church?"

"They were converts to the Church. Very sound, worthwhile people. Hey, they gave me the benefit of every doubt. Mother used to caution me, 'Heavenly Father keeps His eye on you, but do you keep your eye upon Him?'

She worried about me all the time because I challenged her at every turn. What about you? Don't tell me *you* weren't rebellious when you were a tyke."

21

Ruth pictured her mother, a modest soul, thoughtful of others, busy with her artwork and her church callings, but more ambitious for her daughter's future.

"You're the perfect daughter," her mother often said. "I know, don't you, that success is just waiting for you? You're going to make me so proud!"

But Ruth felt that would not happen, not this year or any other. She felt powerless to change her life. Just get through it, she always told herself. It all went back to the day her father left. She remembered him packing his things after that last argument with her mother, who was so upset she left the house. Ruth ran after her.

"You can talk it out," she cried out. "It doesn't have to end like this."

But her mother was unyielding, and when they returned home her father was gone. Ruth ran through the rooms looking for him, then outside to catch him, but it was no use.

When he resettled he wrote her often for awhile, but eventually that stopped, too. Years later Ruth decided that he had abandoned them. She tried to forgive him, to forgive them both, but a stern new quietude grew within her, more of a desolation. Whatever she could become, her heart knew, it would never bring him back.

"I was the compliant one, actually. My parents were very unhappy with their marriage and I guess I just tried to be there for them. Rebellion would have made the whole situation a lot more difficult."

Marshall nodded. "I can easily understand. Sometimes we are brought to a situation so we can be that buffer. Unfortunately, we also get to absorb a lot of the pain of others into ourselves."

On a shelf above him was a replica of a wooden canoe. Marshall took it down and handed it to Ruth.

"It's made of birch. Northwest Indian tribes made their boats with that wood for several hundred years. Strong. They're the best canoes you can find. One like that held me the day my life changed forever."

22

He noted the respect with which she touched the boat and he was grateful she was there with him to share in his remembrances. Ruth turned the boat over. Stained with a lustrous lacquer, it lay in her hands like a jewel.

"It's beautiful, it really is," she whispered. It was like a cradle. A beginning. Can a person begin again, she wondered? She wondered at the careful way the staves fit perfectly together at the bottom of the hull. When her parents split up her own life fell apart. She had never been able to fit those pieces together again. Was it possible? Marshall's energy for life surprised her, and made her think. It was like a small glow of energy that came from far off and moved around her, looking for an entrance. When he spoke of his daring, his love and passion for life, Ruth felt a new stirring.

For a moment they both watched the madronas swaying serenely beyond the window. Neither of them heard Mrs. Willow come softly in to bring them tea and announce that their dinner was getting cold. She moved around to Marshall's chair, sweetly chastising him for sitting too long, refilling his water glass and cleaning away their luncheon plates of hours past.

"Here now, cousin. Take your pills and your swallow of water. Dinner's on the table for you two. You can start your taping again next time."

She was fussing and patting him and Ruth thought that the care she gave him had taught her to love him. As they sat down to dinner she watched Mrs. Willow's busy hands as they cut his meat and poured his tea. She guessed those sure hands had for many years cut potatoes for his stew, changed the sheets on his special hospital bed, tended their overflowing garden and generally washed and cared for him with solemn dedication. After dinner Ruth watched them help each other back down the hall to softer sitting places where Mrs. Willow made her oldest relative another cup of lemon and ginger tea to stimulate his blood and restore that old boyhood flash of a grin she loved so well.

The moon was mixed with amber in prophecy of a lovely day ahead as Ruth drove the highway home. The air, still warm from summer's breath, beckoned her and she pulled off the highway onto a service road that ran along the shore. The tide was out. She walked through the sand, recalling another time so long ago on a beach like this one, when her dad and mom were together. That was when life was fair game. It was not until her father left her that the music became discordant and she could not bear to think of them together any more. Tonight, however, Ruth stayed a long time, lost in thought, until the night's chill broke her reverie.

Four

Ruth drove out of town, heading for Marshall's place. She passed the school where she taught, the grocery where she shopped. She knew everyone there, it seemed she knew every corner of every shop she frequented. Hundreds of faces were familiar to her, they were like stanchions, defining the limits of the tiny territory she called her home. Like her, the population was quiet and steady. Not a few inhabitants were older folks whose recent ancestors trudged west by wagon and sailed north on bold new steamers many years before to get away from the cities.

Many were of Mormon pioneer persuasion, a remnant whose ancestors made that killing trek five generations past to gratefully settle in along the marshy inlets and bays that lined the shore, and from these folk she was descended. The branches of their lives grew long, crossed and crossed again, so that they sometimes forgot who was family and who was not. That brought them closer, and between the teeming saltwater shores and the lush forests of evergreens and firs that both shelter and isolate, they fished the bounty of the sea where winter weather is the principal tenant.

The townspeople, separated in their daily routines and lifestyles by inclination and habit, were also separated in their worship when weekends arrived. They were no different in this way than in millions of towns throughout the world. Passing each other in cars on their way to separate places of worship, the inhabitants lived like the different species of fish caught in the frigid waters of the sea around them.

Watching their habitual weekend routines one could observe that they seemed like unconnected islands in a common ocean. Those who led them in prayer and scripture always spoke of unity and of the love of God that transcends all barriers and should unite all people in "one Lord, one faith, one baptism." But few times in recent memory had one person attended another's church, and rarely was anyone found in church by mistake. Always and ever through the workday week the common bond of friendship was served, but when day is done each soul pulled his life in like a net, straining toward the security of the familiar and the obvious.

Each weekend the people of the town emptied themselves at predetermined doors of worship according to the echoes of their heritage or inclination, and there upon wooden seats or padded pews, within incense-filled halls or the stained cedar walls of a chapel, listening to choirs or chants, testimonies of Jesus Christ or Hebraic rituals, they were among the faces of the familiar and they were content. From such a society of sameness Ruthann Mirra had emerged. In such an atmosphere it was easy to be lulled into spiritual sleep.

This was, in fact, Ruth's only secret shame, for just as she had once trembled with anticipation looking into the eyes of Jesus' likeness, so in the ordinariness of her life she had come to feel estranged from him. This change was not a sudden revelation, over time Ruth noticed in herself doubts of things she always knew were true. She socialized less at lunch with the other administrators and teachers, preferring her own silent company at school rather than to mix with the other teachers.

She could point to no specific reason why she began to demur in prayer, why she neglected to acknowledge Him in all things. When in Church it came time for testimonies, she inexplicably held back. Her beloved scriptures languished, they lay far from her reading lamp, unopened. Her prayer time became reserved for the sacrament portion of Sundays, if at all. The business of living for work consumed her hours. What was it she longed for? She could not recall what was amiss, but more than once she awoke in a sweat from some unremembered dream, hearing her name called.

"Yes," she answered. "I am here!" But only silence.

Sometimes Ruth experienced a vague feeling that something was lost, but in her haste for work and appointments to be kept, she couldn't remember what it was.

Part Two: Maiden Voyage

Five

Ruth's week had been a hard one. Her cold still had her clutching Kleenex for dear life. The paper trail from the classroom to her small home hadn't ceased with summer break. She was pressed to teach classes to cover for a departing colleague, but hated it. His classes were full of disinterested students taking English on a pass/fail basis, a concept popular at the time with administration and parents, but Ruth found the method did not challenge students to learn. That job was up to her.

She found herself eager to see Marshall again. His boyish manner, his incisive memory and buoyant energy were a welcome distraction. Ruth was growing curious to find out what he had hidden from his family most of his long life. Who was the woman in the snapshot above his desk? What significance was there in the little compass? The canoe? Surely he would talk about his marriage and career?

The return trip to Marshall's home was filled with scenes and smells of crisp summer on the Sound. Clouds were white cotton floating high over a cobalt sea, lapping idyllically in the white sun. Gulls seemed to ride the waves, ducking for fish and bickering loudly at scavenging crows and at each other's catches. Marshall and Mrs. Willow had just arrived home when Ruth drove up.

"Hello, there, shorty!" Marshall greeted her. "Wonderful to see you. Just finished my little hike for the day!"

"And before his visit to the doctor for a battery of tests," chimed in Mrs. Willow, taking some things into the house. "If that doctor only knew what Marsh will do to pretend he's twenty. Come in for tea, dear. We'll have scones today, too, nice blackberries."

"Why were you at the doctor's?"

Ruth felt some worry over this news, though she reasoned it might have been only a checkup. She found it difficult to imagine that he was sick and easy to romanticize, to imagine him on the sea, working with ships, though he hadn't yet talked to her about his career or any exploits on the water.

"We have no time now for all that background stuff," he said when she asked about his past. "We'll do that later. I live on time the Lord "sends by mail". I relish each hour, each day, don't you? Life is a gift, Ruth, full of fresh possibilities. Every day we unwrap a little more of our gift. What do you think of that?"

Ruth, always absorbed in detail, asked again about his visit to the doctor. With some reluctance Marshall told her he was being monitored for some heart problems.

"But it's mostly old age. The sawbones says I'm fine, a bit winded, but fine. Still one more voyage in this old ship!"

Marshall clamped an arm across her shoulders and let her help him into the house. He didn't want to frighten her with the news he'd received. What if she became skittish and changed her mind about the interviews, or hesitated to take the helm when the time would come to finish the story despite all odds? He felt gratitude for her willingness and her efforts in his behalf and he thanked Heavenly Father for sending her to him.

30

She sneezed, then groaned.

"Allergies giving your nose a battle? You're the one who needs a doctor, not me. Better hold up, matey, we have work to do." Pointing his cane like a spear he forged the way for them down the long hallway to his study. "That's your office, too, the captain's quarters. Let's get you comfortable. We're going to be here a long time."

He helped her set out the equipment for recording and note taking, showing great pains to make sure she was comfortable before he went to his desk.

Notes: August 6:

"This next section is where miracles begin to happen to me, Ruth. For the record, now, I want my all my grandchildren's children to know that their great grandfather lost his way for a while, but he surely found it again. In those early years I was a boat adrift. When there's no rudder, there's no purpose! But there is always hope in the Lord's direction. God found me in the thickets of my life and steadied me as I faltered, and saved me. That is the story I must pass along.

"I had other valuable teachers. My father was a great man to me. He taught by example. He was a hard worker and a happy man. Never said a lot. Worked in a fishery as an accountant, burning the midnight oil there in his office for years, but sometimes we got lucky. After school sometimes I'd meet him and we'd go fishing down at the pier, just us fellers. Sometimes he read to me. My favorite Book of Mormon story was about Nephi and his wayward brothers. I guess Nephi was a hero to me because I saw him as someone who made his own way in life and didn't stray from it. Unfortunately, I didn't see that the reason for his singleness of purpose was not the same as mine. I refused to read scripture, I fell asleep in church, didn't care a whit for what they tried to teach me there. But there's a lesson in that, young lady. It took me a long time but I finally learned that before Nephi could do those special works which he was commanded by the Lord to do, it took him many years of preparation. He grew in faith. It didn't come all at once. Let me show you something."

Marshall reached for a book that was sandwiched in with several others on the subject of waterways. He opened it to a photograph of clouds above a watery landscape.

"I remember one night. I was just five and very determined to have my own way. I refused to go to bed and instead sneaked outside. I lay on the grass and watched the stars glitter. The time was right for a voyage!" Marshall showed the picture to Ruth.

"This reminds me of those grand times. The mountains were like giant bodies floating on the water. Stars were places to visit. A tip of moon was all you could see. I was aboard my imaginary vessel, a real sailing ship, headed across the water on the way to far off countries. I wanted to see the tail of Halley's Comet on the horizon or maybe a meteor shower. I forgot all about my duties and my lessons. I felt that wind whip around me. Matey, I *knew* there were mysteries across the world just calling me to investigate."

Marshall laughed at this. "I fell asleep on the grass, spread out like a star. My dad found me there and woke me up, busting up my dream. Wasn't sorry I'd been caught outside past my bedtime, not at all. I disobeyed my father so many times, but he was always there for me. It's funny, when you know your parents are going to love you no matter what, you can be yourself with them, your best and your worst self, and I was at my worst a lot of the time. I could get away with spending long hours outside in all kinds of weather, didn't need much sleep. I'd stuff lunch in my stolen backpack, sneak down the stairs, slip out the back door to freedom. My parents rarely knew where I was. Couldn't resist the call to adventure. Oh, I was firmly unrepentant for a long time. Why, if I hadn't met the fellers I'm going to tell you about I'd have gone to my grave a criminal. I'm sure of that, sure as salt about that."

That describes me, Ruth thought as she watched the tape recorder wind Marshall's words into memory. Maybe I'm a drifting boat in the "thickets" of my life, too. Uneasiness came

32

over her, so much so that she excused herself to find Mrs. Willow.

"I'll just get this teapot refilled." Marshall, sensing her uneasiness, rose with her.

"You know, Ruth, we can discuss anything you want. This time we have isn't just my time, but yours, too. Have I said something that troubles you?"

Ruth smiled hesitantly. How could she tell this relative stranger her deepest thoughts?

"No, no. Nothing, really. We can go on. It's nothing. Be right back."

Swiftly, she left the room. Marshall, watching her go, knew that his words had somehow touched her. For the first time, he was seeing a little beneath her calm surface and he knew she was working something out within herself. Time divulges its mysteries, he thought darkly. He hoped she would take him into her confidence eventually. When she returned, Marshall said:

"Ruth, I really appreciate your willingness to record my special story. How do you feel about it, so far?" His eyes searched her countenance for clues.

Ruth was honest with him, choosing her words carefully.

"It's such an interesting story. I know we've just gotten started but I'm really looking forward to hearing about your experiences. There may even be a lesson in it for me," she smiled ruefully. Well, it's possible, she told herself.

"I hope it touches your heart, dear. It profoundly changed my own. When I met those mates I was really confused. Looking back now I'd say I wasn't aware of anything outside myself. Remember the Hebrew prophet, Jeremiah? He wrote about those *empty cisterns*. He meant that life without the love of God holds nothing. I was looking for happiness in my own pleasures. I just followed my own rebellious path."

Marshall looked out the window at the bay's calm.

"It was on the raging sea where I discovered for myself that our Savior, Jesus Christ, is the true vessel that holds the living water. He filled the empty cistern of my stubborn heart."

He smiled broadly and studied Ruth for another minute, feeling that his words had helped in some way he didn't know.

33

Her shoulders relaxed. She settled back in her chair and looked at the canoe.

"Now, by my thirteenth year my situation had become a strain for everyone. I wouldn't take the sacrament in Church and that gave my parents much anxiety. They took me to counseling with our bishop, who I really liked. But it was hard to obey anyone. It seemed I was always restricted to my room, where I hated to be. Everything that could be done for me, my parents did, but I didn't want any of it. I felt like I was being jailed for doing what I loved.

Marshall dug into a desk drawer and brought out a weathered book. It's binding was old and torn, as though it has been packed in many a box, pushed and pulled between stacks of other books. The covers were a battleship gray with raised black markings. It strongly resembled a type of business ledger used many years ago, printed with lines of blue and red upon a cheap ragweed stock. With a smile Marshall handed Ruth the book.

"This is my real treasure," he said, his voice deepening. On the cover in flourish black script were the words "*My Journal*". On the inside page, along with the date 1913 in bold pen and ink script, was his name, with the words "*Captain of The Press On.*" Ruth opened it and stared at the quill-like penmanship and the boldly written words almost sunken into the old paper.

"That's my *first* journal. Bought after my initial encounter with the angels. All that has happened, all of our talks and journeys are in those pages. Now, you're the first to see it other than myself. We'll use this record as we progress. That way, your information can be accurate. Sound good?"

He laughed in triumph, like a fisherman who caught a big one and lived to tell the story.

Ruth was intrigued. Turning the pages she saw they were filled with descriptions of the sea. There were dialogues and whimsical drawings of what appeared to be angels, terse notations and various lists of scriptural references. Words were scrawled hurriedly in old blue ink, many preceded and followed by dashes. The journal was more like a series of memory prompts than a coherent story line. Marshall's grammar was basic. It made the strange notations the more believable. She

34

felt an old excitement return to her as she read. It was like a ship's log, filled with description, reactions, discoveries. This book was an antique, a genuine relic. But Marshall put out his hand for it. Reluctantly, she gave it back.

"I'm sorry." I don't want you getting ahead of me. This is meat, not milk. When I give up my ghost, it becomes part of my estate, but for now it will be our guide to discovery!

"It's fantastic. Is that your record of the story you're going to tell?"

Marshall set the frayed old journal before him and opened it to the first page.

"It is. The very one. Ah, this takes me back. One day in school I got in a mean scrape with another boy. He called me a ruffian, a good-for-nothing. That got me good and angry and I brought my anger home with me. Mother couldn't do anything with me. She sent me to bed right after dinner, which made me even angrier. I eventually fell asleep, but I was restless."

"I must have started to dream, because suddenly I saw a very tall man wearing white robes. He walked toward me. When he got close he called my name. I thought he told me not to be afraid, but I was startled anyway. His clothes were white, but not like bedsheets. This white was like a star up close. It came from his very self, like some energy I'd never seen. He glowed."

"I can tell you I was really scared. I opened my mouth to tell him to leave, but he smiled at me. Then he laughed. Instead of fear, a sweet peacefulness came over me. This was no ghost, mind you, he was real and he looked like a man. His skin and hair were of a brilliance that was blinding. His total frame radiated so intensely that I closed my "dream" eyes to avoid the glare.

"While I was trying to decide what to do next, he spoke to me. His voice was strong and deep, but genuinely kind, and his words seemed to come from within myself. They were more like thoughts than language. They *sang* in my ears, too, like an echo. I heard everything twice. I was too amazed to do anything. I wrote down his first words to me:

"I have come on a special errand: to teach thee the meaning of love and the words of life. Thou needs to be restored to thy childlike state through repentance, from thy current state of sin to true happiness."

"This white figure talked like someone who was used to giving orders, like a captain or an administrator. I was still in shock. Then he reminded me that my parents had tried to teach me truth from error (and it was true) but I always found something else to catch my attention. When they gave me the Bible or the Book of Mormon to read I fell asleep over it. When they lectured me on my duties, I walked away. None of the teachers in the Church had much hope for gaining my attention, either, because I was always dreaming and scheming how I could get away, go on an adventure, become a whaler or a pirate, or discover Antarctica. The last thing that interested me was learning about prophets or reading scriptures. That was, to me, a huge waste of time."

"My visitor also told me that in answer to my parents' many petitions, God had sent a pair of His angels as teachers to my spirit. He assured me that they were holy angels of God and he extended his hand to shake mine. I hesitated a long time, let me tell you. How often do you shake the hand of an angel? It felt solid to my touch."

Marshall shook his head, reliving his wonder and disbelief. He was there again, in his dream, seeing again the whiteness of his visitor, hearing once more the echoing sound of his words.

"Always had dreams, you know, but never like that. My dreams were about climbing mountains and going to sea or building the big ships. But this was a new world. Now I do also recall that the area around this "angel" was glowing white. It near blinded me, yet I felt love and peace in his presence. It was the strangest thing, but I wasn't afraid.

"He must have read my mind. He told me that dreams can be our way of seeing far into the future of our lives, even into the eternities, like a window opened. 'There is a world that exists outside thy daily lives and understanding. When thou are allowed to look within that other world thou can see thy own spirit's quest for greater meaning.' He spoke very quietly to my spirit. Somehow, when he spoke to me like that, I understood him. I guess I stopped being scared at that point and settled down a little.

"'It is time for thee to meet my companion, Barak. Actually, Marshall, thou may refer to us as Silas and Barak. I am Silas, the tall one.'" And here he smiled again and laughed as if the joke was on him. 'God always sends his missionary angels by two's that we may share the burdens and joys of teaching human spirits.'

I found my voice a little bit and tried to talk with this fellow.

"If you are angels, how did you get here? I didn't ask for you. And where are your wings?"

Being a streetwise, stubborn kid, I wasn't going to give in easily to these strange beings. I knew this was all my parents' doing. But I was also starting to think that maybe I really was going to get in trouble.

"Silas came closer to me. He smiled. Would you believe that even his teeth glowed?"

'We are here by the grace and direction of our Father in Heaven who made the universes and all that in them are, and we may come to thee in thy world of day, as it befits our purpose to guide thee onto the path of God.'

"'Thou may not be aware of thy quest for truth, but thy Father in heaven who made thee in His image, He knows thee and the needs of thy heart. *There is none else save God that knowest thy thoughts and the intents of thy heart.*' He touched my shoulder but I didn't pull back. 'God loves thee very much, Marshall, but thou are quite sure thine own way is best. God has sent us to show thee a better way.' He laughed in a deep voice. 'Thou has asked about our wings. The holy angels of God are not given wings but are of flesh and bone. These appendages thou calls wings and which earth's artists fancifully draw are not of us. Our power to move comes from Heavenly Father alone.'"

"Silas had no sooner said 'our' than I saw a short, rather pudgy figure coming toward us. He was glowing, too. He shook Silas' hand. They both turned to me.

"'This is my companion, who we will call Barak. It means *lightening*. Say hello to Marshall, thou Barak.'

37

"Barak put out his white hand to me and I shook it. Yep, he was real, all right. He smiled so brightly I couldn't look directly at either one of them. I knew I was going to wake up blinded.

"So happy to meet you, young sir," he said with great affection. I felt myself becoming very calm inside as he said it. He reminded me of my mother, whose sweetness never seemed to leave her. It always caught people off guard.

"Silas told Barak of our meeting. He outlined the task ahead of me. Barak beamed at me and shook his head with great vigor. 'Right, right, right,' he nodded. 'And shall we be starting tonight?' he inquired of Silas.

Six

"They both studied me intently. The aura around them was several inches wide at every point. It pulsed as they spoke. I began to fiddle with my clothes, something I do when I'm nervous. Remember the scripture that tells how to identify God's angels? I did, but I was still unconvinced, never having met one - I mean two- in a dream before."

"Silas must have read my thoughts." He stared at me.

'Would thou like to pray and ask thy Father in Heaven if we are really sent by Him to thee?' Barak nodded his agreement for me.

'Good, good. *But when they in their trouble did turn unto the Lord god of Israel, and sought him, he was found of them.* God answers prayers. We hope thou will pray night and day.'

"They had me there. I had prayed years ago for answers to questions about God, but I never really knew if they were answered. Maybe this time it would be different. Of course, I was real curious to know if these 'angels' were from God (and if I had to listen to them). I said it would be okay. 'But *you* have to do the praying," I said.

"'Fine. That's a good decision, my child,' Barak said gleefully. 'We will all ask Him to make His desires for thee known. Dost thou remember the proper order of prayer?'

"I did remember. I had been taught to fold my arms, bow my head and begin by saying 'Dear Heavenly Father.' Then I had to thank Him for my blessings before I could ask for anything. When I was done I had to close in the name of Jesus Christ and say 'amen.'"

That part was easy. The angels closed their eyes and folded their arms. Their gowns rustled, like they were standing in the wind. They gave off bright little flashes of lightening. It was something like the Northern Lights over Alaska, but all in white. I bowed my head, but kept my eyes on them.

"Silas offered the prayer. Over the course of our time together these angels prayed for me many times. He spoke the words and I listened, but I was not ready for what I heard. Silas thanked God for sending them to me, for making the universes, the earth, the sea, the stars, for making me and my family. Then he thanked God for so many more things that it took a long time just to finish that part. Eventually, he asked that my heart would be softened so I could learn what they had come to teach me. He asked for a blessing upon my parents and grandparents. Just when I thought he was going to wind it up he again fell to praising God. In the middle of his praising he switched to another language like it was the most natural thing to do. I couldn't understand a word he said, but Barak solemnly nodded in agreement, his head bowing lower.

"When the prayer was finished, Silas turned to me and gave me another name, but immediately forbid me to say it anywhere but in my thoughts, so that it would never be heard by a human voice. Even now I must protect it, but it's a really strange one. They said it comes from a language spoken only in Heaven. 'We will call thee Marshall only and thou may call us by Silas and Barak only, as these were our earth names long ago. In this way it is guaranteed that nothing sacred will be revealed. Dost thou agree?' Well, I had to agree. At that point I was so amazed at them and what I call their *gleamyness* that I would have agreed to about anything.

"Has thy prayer been answered yet in thy heart?" Barak asked me enthusiastically. He seemed always on the verge of jumping for joy.

"Not yet. Maybe God is busy."

"'He is never too busy to answer heartfelt prayers, Marshall. God always answers the prayers of the heart. He finds thy heart within thee and speaks to it in love forevermore. *My son, if thou wilt receive my words, and hide my commandments with thee; so that thou incline thine ear to wisdom, and apply thine heart to understanding.* Dost thou have the faith to receive an answer?'

"Faith. There he had found my weak spot. That was one of the things they lectured about in church, but I never really listened.

"'I have faith…well, some. Faith has never worked for me much. Do we have to do this right now?'"

40

"But these fellers just smiled again. One thing they had was happiness. It was always there, shining from their eyes. They reminded me of my grandmother's eyes, soft pale blue."

"'Our God has sent us to thee, little one. Your lessons must begin soon, very soon. There will be time enough for thee to receive strong testimony of us as thy God-sent teachers. As for now, we have terms to discuss. Art thou willing to be taught the lessons of love and life by God's holy angels?'"

Marshall stopped reading and looked up at Ruth. She was leaning forward, listening to every word. Her eyes were bright and Marshall saw an intensity in them, as though she were there with him and the angels, anticipating every word. As he looked at her, she seemed to sense her own involvement and sat back with a slight smile, like she'd been caught at something.

"That's amazing," she whispered, feeling her cheeks getting hot. "Forgive me, Brother Cannon, but, well, ah, I was just wondering if this is a true story?"

Marshall sat up in surprise. He hadn't considered that she might not believe him.

"It's as real as we are sitting here, young lady. My, yes, it all happened just as I wrote it here - "

He jabbed a finger into the spine of the book.

"You don't believe it?"

Ruth recoiled. She had upset him. She looked at the floor, trying to figure out what to say next. It was all so *different*, so, well, *unbelievable*!

"I'm sorry, I really think it's a wonderful story, but how can angels appear like that, in dreams, I mean."

Marshall looked at the compass before him on the desk, and at the canoe, remembering the storm that nearly took his life. What would it take to convince this child of the miracles of God?

Suddenly the tape recorder clicked to signal the end of the tape. Mrs. Willow appeared, as if on cue, with more hot tea water for Ruth and a glass of fresh water for Marshall. He smiled at her tenderly and she patted his shoulder, passing Ruth a wink as she left. Ruth was starting to love them both.

Marshall waited until Mrs. Willow left the room and then he said

41

"You know, when I was a boy and went to the sea, the world drew me in and the words of the Lord were lost in the wind. I was like a blind man I once encountered with a dark cane a lot like this one. Spiritual blindness. It's like being on Alaskan waters at night, unable to see the tips of icebergs or judge distances. The water looks safe as long as you think there are no obstacles ahead and you assume you can handle whatever happens. I think that's a common problem with people, don't you? What we cannot see ceases to exist for us, yet more is beyond the view of our eyes than this world contains, often dangerous times, and it's easy to lose our way."

"But the Lord always allows u-turns. He wants us to follow *Him*, for He can see the trouble ahead better than we can. The question for each of us is, how enlightened must our walk of faith become before our crutches can be left behind and we depend entirely on him?"

Marshall turned to his bookcase. After a moment he dislodged a volume and laid it on the desk. It was the LDS publication of the Holy Bible. On top of it he put his Book of Mormon. On top of that he laid his right hand.

"This is my proof. These are holy books, books of eternal truth. For most of my life I have tried mightily to live by the words in these books. Now I tell you that these things you are hearing are true, and I leave you with my testimony of them in the sacred name of Jesus Christ, amen. I suggest also that when you return to your home tonight you pray to know for yourself whereof I speak."

He sat down again and turned to the next page of his journal, waiting for Ruth to turn on the tape recorder.

It was the turning point of their relationship. The old man and the young woman, coming to terms over the essential question of believability. It was a question that begged solving and nothing less would do. Marshall wanted with all of his failing heart for this young woman to believe him, to share his wonder at being ministered to by angels of the Lord. All these years he hadn't told but one soul because he was afraid his family wouldn't believe him. He had to face the probability that they'd think it just some childish fantasy. Ruth was his last hope, she was young and unbiased. Maybe she'd come to share his love for the miracles that changed his life, but if she didn't believe, then why would anyone else? Maybe it was all a wasted effort. He'd just destroy the damned journal and carry his secret to his grave.

He looked over his journal at her. Ruth was still, sitting with her eyes closed, not knowing what to say. So it was true, he did not suffer from hallucinations or delusions. It was true, not just a strange and entertaining story, but fact. She knew it now. She felt it borne to her in his testimony. She shook her head. Strange but true, okay. Fine, let's continue, she said to herself. Then she looked at Marshall and smiled widely and said it aloud.

"Fine. Let's continue, before we lose precious time." And she turned on the tape recorder.

"Think about it. How many mortals have ever been asked if they'll be taught the Gospel of Christ by angels? I was in a unique position to answer and many thoughts passed through my mind. First, did I want to learn? There were responsibilities that went with the doctrine they would teach (I was not entirely deaf to my scripture training). I was also afraid my new study would keep me from the bayfront, and all my other favorite haunts. I was working on a third reason for my hesitancy when Barak spoke."

"'Heavenly Father has told us that you want to be a sailor. What a wonderful thing! I love to sail through the heavens from planet to planet. There is so much to see and do. So much to learn about the worlds our God has made. What happiness and joy there is in learning about our Father's work. We could share some of it with thee, if thou were to agree…'"

"One thing there is about angels, Ruth. They know what to say and when and how it should be said. I knew they could teach me a lot. They probably knew where treasure lay beneath the sea, where the biggest fish bite, how planes stay in the air, and where barges and ships go when they seem to fall off the horizon. But, deep down, something else nagged at me. Truth was, I didn't like myself much the way I was. Just that day some guy I thought was my friend called me a 'jerk'. In addition to that, I was caught stealing and spent a night at my bishop's house while he read to me from the Book of Mormon. Don't forget the problems with my parents. That was serious. What did I have to lose? I told them I'd give it a go."

"Barak actually did jump up and down twice, and Silas, he was the more dramatic of the two, he put his hands together and sighed just like all his wishes had come true. I sighed, too. I looked around and a seat appeared. I sat down heavily to acknowledged my defeat. My parents had won. Maybe God really did want me to learn about - how did they put it - the 'words of life.' One thing I knew for sure about God. He was smarter than me."

"My teachers didn't waste any time in giving me the terms of our 'classroom' sessions. I would agree to receive their 'ministrations' for the time *they* thought necessary for my spiritual education. During that time they promised to explain the ways of the kingdom of God in Heaven, and they said they'd help me discover my true purpose on the earth. They assured me that joyfulness would come into my life. In addition, they would answer questions about the sea, the stars, ships, etc. They also promised that I would advance greatly in faith and knowledge which, if properly noted and remembered, would 'accompany thee through thy long life and be a wondrous blessing upon thee, thy family and thy posterity.' If I wanted to learn more, they were there to teach me. I would also be free to deep six the whole shebang at any time."

"But, this little plan of theirs had its price. I had to take notes, something I hate doing, and be prompt for every discussion. I had to agree to pray to know the truthfulness of their teachings, I had to ask to pass the sacrament in church and read my scriptures *every day*. I could not take trips anywhere without first asking my parents, and I had to clean my room and do chores when asked. Those were their terms. Boy, they were hard. I thought about each of those things for a long time. They knew I'd give in. They weren't worried, but I sure was."

Marshall laughed aloud at the memory. He reached again for his Bible.

Trust in the Lord with all thine heart; and lean not unto thine own understanding. In all thy ways acknowledge him, and he shall direct thy paths...My son, despise not the chastening of the LORD; neither be weary of his correction; (Proverbs 3:5,6,11)

"I couldn't believe my ears! They had me at every turn. They knew exactly what I was up to and what was to be done. I was trapped! Ask my parents for permission to skip school? Give up spelunking and fishing and stay in class? Read scripture *every day*? They were asking me to *change my life*! How could I accept those terms? I wanted to cry. But, you know, somewhere deep in my heart I must have agreed, because I remember shaking hands with them to seal the bargain, and I remember their smiles of victory, too."

"Barak said 'Great, great, good. Good decision. But time for us to go. Silas and I, thy Heaven-sent angels of love, must leave thee now and do so with thy Heavenly Father's love, in the name of Jesus Christ, amen. Meetings to be off to. We give thee the sleep of angels now, Marshall. We will visit thee again soon.' And they were gone. I was still in awe of them, but pretty soon I felt tired and heavy. I slept so deeply that night I was late to school next morning, but thankfully no one noticed."

Marshall sat back and took a sip of his water. It was much easier now that she believed him. He was thankful she'd been forthright in speaking her mind. Now a calm sweet spirit was in the room. Ruth stopped the tape recorder and reviewed her own notes. She knew he was being spiritually fed by his memory of these two angels who became beloved friends. Tears are in his reddened eyes, she wrote. I think they are tears of love and gratitude. She passed Marshall the tissue box. And then she smiled at him, a warm, genuine smile.

Seven

David, Marshall Cannon's great grandson, came to class late, as he had numerous times, but his demeanor was always sweet and repentant. Ruth's biting chastisement had fewer teeth in it than usual this day. She wanted to ask him about his great grandfather. He quickly referred her to his mother with the news that he had not known "Gramps Cannon" long or spent much time in his company. The old man had been a traveler, it seemed, often spending months and even years out of state in pursuit of interests which David had no knowledge of, other than to say that "Gramps" gave away money and sometimes had to fly across the world to deliver it. That evening Ruth phoned David's mother, Jewel.

"I'm so glad you called," her pleasant voice said in my ear. "Grandpa Cannon is the sweetest man and we just love him so much! Are you feeling better? Claudia so enjoyed meeting you and she said you were having a cold. I was under the weather, too, you know, these allergies can be such a pain! Are you still sick? How is Grandpa Cannon doing?"

Ruth assured her that he was robust. She thanked Jewel for choosing her to record "Grandpa Cannon's" memoirs, but told her nothing of their interviews. "He is a fascinating man and I really enjoy listening to him," she said.

Jewel's personality bubbled back. There were so many things she wanted to share with oldest son David's English teacher about his schoolwork, his eating habits, homework habits, sleep patterns, her husband's sudden lack of eating breakfast syndrome, school papers, David's grades, ad infinitum. When finally she had to cough, Ruth asked her about her grandfather's early life. Jewel paused a moment, as if reluctant to talk about it directly.

"We don't know a lot about Grandpa Cannon. He's a very private man. Margaret, my mother, always checks up on him. Naida, his wife, was from the Yukon, you know. Grandpa Cannon has had a very long and busy life, but few of us know much about him. He probably won't tell you very much, either, but please get what you can."

Jewel sounded really apologetic. Her comments only intensified Ruth's curiosity. She could offer scant detail.

"Grandpa Cannon is very independent. He hasn't even been back in the northwest here for too long, maybe fifteen years. He was in a war, I forget which one, but it was a long time ago. I've only been to his home only occasionally, though I do recall seeing some medals on a living room shelf there, but you know me and medals!"

An image came to Ruth of Jewel hurriedly turning over his ribboned awards as if they were incomprehensible objects.

"The one to ask is my aunt, my mother's only sister. Mother died shortly after my birth. Aunt Sylvia was always kind of special to Grandpa Cannon. I'm sure she knows a lot that she hasn't told anyone."

Ruth took the phone number, determined to follow up in a day or two. Supposing that Marshall Cannon had been "in retirement" for fifteen years, most of his lifetime was still unaccounted for. Was the photo in his study of Naida? What was it that took him away for months and years at a time? As for medals, he'd had time to soldier in numerous wars. Was he a war hero? A simple request to record a memoir was becoming a tantalizing quest to uncover a growing mystery.

Ruth's next trip to Marshall's home was in the evening. She'd found she loved to drive the coast at sundown. Clouds were strewn across the air like a peninsula, here and there penetrated by light that fell finally on the water in alternating grays, so that the sea held that somber brightness, returning a hue that resembled slow moving concrete. The ever present gulls floated above on wind currents, then expertly landed on the V's of housetops, where they burnished their wings and listened to the music of the sea. Trees bristled on the shores of islands beyond the haze. Night was still hidden in the air but already the arc of the moon was in readiness.

Sometimes she drove to the bay just to sit and watch it, the way the sea responds to the changing tides while everything else seems stationary. This evening she thought of the Savior who

48

walked the moving waters at will, calming the storm, commanding the elements. Suddenly, she longed to know her own heart. She wanted to restore Marshall to his youth and former energy. She wanted greater understanding of angelic visits to mortals. Were they a fiction of the heart or truly humanity's (mostly) unseen guides, patient ministers to our foolish, independent spirits? Part of a scripture from Moroni when he taught of the Lord to the Lamanites, came to her:

...they who have faith in him will cleave unto every good thing; wherefore he advocateth every good thing;... and because he hath done this, my beloved brethren, have miracles ceased? Behold I say unto you, Nay; neither have angels ceased to minister unto the children of men. For behold, they are subject unto him...

Many scriptures teach that holy angels are sent of God to man, to do His bidding, though often unbidden and even unwelcome by mortal recipients. Faith, of course, is the keyword that unlocks all heavenly business. Ruth's bishop had told her that. Many who receive manifestations are not aware of their own faith or that they crave more faith, but the Lord knows their hearts, he told her when she admitted one day that her faith was not strong. Ruth *felt* that Marshall was being truthful in the telling of his experiences. He surely had dreamed what he said he dreamed, as have so many others through time. It was as real to *him* as any experience he'd known, and now she knew also that it was a true record, and she envied him his undoubting faith in the Gospel. But where was his story leading? What was the secret he had kept from everyone these long years of his life? Finally, beneath all her wondering was the ever present question that moved in her deepest thoughts like a current beneath the surface of the leaden sea: When will it be my time? Will they ever speak to me?

Marshall was waiting for her at the door. He opened it wide and clamped an arm around her shoulders, joyfully welcoming

Ruth inside. Mrs. Willow had readied homemade citron scones, cheese omelets and hash browns. She set a pot of tea beside them. They were becoming well acquainted now, this trip was Ruth's fifth in four weeks. She loved the easy camaraderie they'd developed. Mrs. Willow discussed replanting the nasturtiums. Marshall wanted more shelves in his study. He apologized with a wink to Ruth for the messy state of "their" office.

"Hey, you're the one with all the books and papers,"

Ruth laughed and winked back. She felt a part of their lives, now, and as they gathered at the table and petitioned the Lord for his blessings she knew that it was indeed he who sent little Claudia to her door in a summer shower to point the way.

In the study after dinner, Marshall gave Ruth some preparatory notes.

"I've been thinking about the thrust of this memoir, my dear. We have to make it clear that these dreams were the most soul changing events I've ever known. My spirit hungered to be taught, and I think that's why Silas and Barak came to me so often. I had to learn to accept the angels as a real force in my life. That took time. I was very rebellious at first. Now, in their quiet way, my parents also had a lot to do with my decision to accept those teachings because they'd prayed for years for something to come along and change me. The trust I had in my mother and father really helped me to *want* to change. It was a decisive move and a wise one, as I look back."

"Now, after every appearance in my dreams, there was a lull in time of several weeks before Silas and Barak appeared to me again. I think they wanted to be sure I could absorb the things they told me and that I wasn't too pressured. Never had anything like that happened in my life. I was actually afraid at first that every time I closed my eyes to rest I would see Barak laughing or Silas with his arms spread out, but they left me to my privacy, I'll say that for them. And they never showed themselves in daylight. So eventually I learned that I really could not ignore the knowledge when it came. After the first few sessions and for the first time in my life I began to seriously examine my thoughts and actions. Once I did that, it was easy to see how my

50

lifestyle was breaking up our family unity and giving my parents grief. It was also leading me down some stony roads.

"Still, it was a struggle because I really did not want to change. It took more time for the Savior to enter my heart because I tried hard to be an ungovernable kid."

Marshall had found some papers stuck in a crack between journal pages. Laboriously he unfolded them.

"An old letter to myself, years ago. Let's see what it says..."

"'It's Saturday morning, dawn has come and gone. I'm already restless. I can smell the sea, the seaweed, the salt. It calls me. Boy, do I want to go fishing! My pole is resting there against the wall, its hook moves in the breeze from my open window. If this were just any weekend I'd be long gone because I always leave home soon after dawn to head for the docks or the river nearby where I know the trout will grab a juicy worm off my hook.'"

"'But this Saturday's different. I told the angels I wouldn't leave the house without permission. What if I don't get it? I can hear Dad humming downstairs. He's up already and working in the barn. I just got back from dad and mom's room. Mom is still asleep. I didn't want to wake her, so I sat on the floor near her side of the bed and watched her sleeping. Does she have dreams like I do? I wonder if she was afraid of the dark when she was a girl. I was afraid a few years ago. Some nights were really scary, especially after I ate candy. My room seemed to fill up with monsters beneath the bed. I know I heard noises in that little closet. Mom and dad always came on the run whenever I screamed.'"

"'That was a long time ago, but I remember it like it just happened. Shucks. I'll never be what my parents or my grandparents or Mrs. Jensen or my bishop see in me. Now angels are giving me counsel! No one understands that I just need to be *me*! Mrs. Jensen in Primary said Alma the prophet spoke with angels. Alma said men were supposed to repent of their wrong doings and he sent angels to talk with them. Are those the angels that visited me?'"

"'Maybe I'll break my agreement with them. Should I tell Mom and Dad about my dream? I know if I do they'll either think I'm crazy or agree with Silas and Barak and I won't be able to go out alone anymore. I don't know what to do.'"

Ruth laughed with Marshall at hearing the letter. She thought of the many times in her life she'd been confused and full of turmoil. It seemed then that her dad and mom had the right answers, but now... the questions were more problematical, the answers a lot harder to come by.

Eight

Marshall put the letter in the book and leaned back in his chair.

"I went downstairs and found my mother asleep. She had a way of counseling me. She lay there so peaceful. Sometimes she'd smile. I used to listen to her breathing, it calmed me, you know? Her breath smelled a little like the wheat that grew behind our barn and I remember so well how I used to cling to her as though she were strong as the earth, as if she were life itself. So many nights she comforted me with her soft breath. She sang hymns of love and hope to me, I'll never forget her doing that. You know *'I Am A Child of God'*? We used to sing it together at my bedtime until my little-boy fears lost their power and I could sleep."

"But my nightmares disappeared eventually. Then I started having dreams of traveling all over the place. In fact, they became a kind of plan of action. I'd wake up remembering them and spend the rest of the day or week living them out. But after I made that agreement with the angels I was really scared I'd get restricted to the house. They wanted me to grow up, to share myself with them, but grown up things still frightened me."

"Oh, I've forgotten this."

He dislodged another paper scrap from between the pages.

"It's a poem of sorts. I was so unhappy that night, I wrote this verse. I've kept it all these years. It's terrible. Want to hear it?"

Ruth leaned forward, her eyes alive with interest.

"Of course. What kind of poem is it?"

"A little boy's wail. Had lots of time on my hands that year."

"*'Oh, what will I become? They expect too much of me.*
Lots of times I think I'm smart. I could take this world apart!
(But sometimes I'm just dumb.)
What should I believe? I sure can get confused.

My parents say the golden rule will keep me from becoming cruel.'"

They say, give but I think, get.
In what direction is my fate? Was I born too soon or late?
Perhaps I'm meant to be a bum and march to my own loud drum.
My father tells me to stand tall -
(But who will catch me when I fall?)'"

"I like that," Ruth said, laughing. "You were quite a mixed up kid. Did you ever tell your parents about the angels?"

"Well, I was going to talk to my mother, but when I found her asleep I thought about spilling the beans to my dad. I found him outside. He gave me a hug and asked me to help him fix our chicken coop and I agreed. I think he sensed I wanted to talk. He asked me if I was going down to the docks again. I sort of mumbled that I wanted to. Boy, I wanted to go so bad I almost shouted it out, but I was trying to be careful. I was so afraid he'd say 'no'. But he really surprised me. He said we could go together and do some fishing after we finished in the barn."

"I think he was trying to *help* me make the decision not to run off. He must have missed me. Dad worked hard for us. Sometimes when he came home he'd be too tired to eat and he'd fall asleep in his chair listening to the radio. I saw new lines in his forehead. He got new glasses. The lenses were really thick. 'That's because of all the small print I have to read,' he told me, but he wore them more and more. He kept a small bottle of pills in his shirt pocket because he had bad headaches. I remember looking at him that day and knowing that I loved him with all my heart.

"While we worked I asked him what he knew about angels. Dad was an elder in the Church with a good knowledge of scripture. He was well read on many subjects and he loved to talk about spiritual things. We usually held Family Home Evenings after they joined the Church, but to me it was always just another chore. Now I was glad we could discuss something.

"'Have you ever seen or talked to an angel?' I asked him. He was startled at that, but he said no, not to his memory."

'Why do you ask?' he wanted to know. I couldn't bring myself to tell him about it, not yet. 'Oh, I just wonder, that's all. Do you think they still talk to people?'

Dad said he was sure they did. He told me that angels are a part of the spirit world and they serve our Heavenly Father.

"'Dreams are made for us, son, so we can work out problems. Sometimes we receive the Spirit of the Lord through our dreams. He sends His Spirit to us for comfort. Of course, there's lots of times when we don't know what our dreams mean. Remember the story of King Nebuchadnezzar in the book of Daniel? He dreamt of an image made of precious metals, iron and clay that suddenly broken apart after being 'smote' by a stone cut out of a mountain without hands.'"

Dad said Daniel had inspiration so he could interpret the king's dream. It was amazing because it predicted that the Gospel would be restored to the earth thousands of years before it came to pass. He was quite a fellow, my dad."

Ruth thought of her own father, loving and gentle with her. He'd always searched her out when he came home from work, just to hug and say hello.

"My dad and I never talked about angels. He would tell me about his work and I'd tell him about some book I found in the library, or about school, little things. We used to walk around the block and discuss them. I still miss him."

"I'm sure he misses you, too, Ruth. Did you ever hear from him after he left your mother?"

"He wrote me for a few months, then he stopped. It's been many years now, but I feel that he's okay. Maybe one day I'll find him again."

She still had his last letter to her and read it often. It was the only lifeline between them now. She thought a minute.

"It seems to me that your basic fight within yourself was over faith. I mean, you didn't have much, then, but you really wanted to believe what your parents and your teachers were telling you. Is that right?"

"You are so right. I did want to trust, but for some reason I just had to do things my own way. They never led to anything good. I always came up against the same problems. It's hard to believe in something you can't see, isn't it?"

Ruth pondered his words. This time she heard them differently. Faith, trust in the truth. Evidence was all around. It was a question of faith.

"I'd sure like to receive angelic revelation, like you did. I wish they would come to me." There, she'd said it. Marshall nodded in understanding.

"Don't hurry it, Ruth. We are each entitled to receive revelation, our prophets have told us that. As your sensitivity to the Spirit of the Lord grows they may well come and visit with you, just don't give up hope. They come in response to your need. Often enough they came to me after that first encounter. But I didn't want them, or thought I didn't. They were like God's policemen, watching me to make sure I didn't sneak out to go fishing or stow away on a fishing boat."

"After a while it really dampened my spirits, because they were teaching me about so many things that I felt myself changing. Every time I wanted to sneak away I felt guilty, though sometimes I didn't let that stop me. Then I started talking more with my folks and listening to the radio with them. They kept asking me if I was all right. I even cleaned my room and washed windows. My mother had me dump the trash and mow the lawn. They made me visit my old aunt." He laughed. "I really felt lost."

"They really changed you, Marshall. They taught you to believe in so many things."

"Yes, and in angels. I did some studying on the subject. Angels can visit us when we need to receive important messages and can't get them any other way. They come to us when nothing else will do and they help us to have greater faith and insight. Nephi was given the vision of our Savior's life and ministry through angelic messages. I was reading in the book of Alma last night after you left. When Alma and Amulek preached the Gospel to Zeezrom, Alma said 'angels were sent to converse' with men to teach them the Plan of Salvation. So, by the power of the Holy Ghost, the people of that time were made aware of the glory of God."

56

"Well, after their third visit several months passed. I was amazed that my memory of them had not faded. Their words still rolled around in my brain. Without realizing at first, I found myself looking for them, waiting and watching. Once, I thought I spotted them in a crowd at the market. Another time I was sure I glimpsed their glowing white gowns on the way to school. But I couldn't be sure.

"Meanwhile, that old urge to be off to the docks was still very strong in me. Truthfully, I did run off again, more times than I'll admit, but much less by comparison. It was a summer like this one. The sun's light made the water shine, the fish were plentiful. Adventure called."

"I had a buddy we called Spank because he was always in trouble, so we named him for the "reward" that usually followed his pranks. He stole an old canoe, it was pretty beat up, and he hid it in the trees at a cove near our house. Few people knew about that place in my childhood days. No roads led to it. It was small, just about seven feet, made of birch. One oar was cracked, but serviceable. It was watertight, but a little rot had invaded the shell and staving. That canoe had taken a lot of battering from many storms. We didn't care. It was better than nothing and it always got us across the Sound to the island all right. We used it in summer and we had a pact that no one of us could steal it or use it without another member of our gang going along."

"In those days more than anything I wanted a boat of my own. Dad and I talked about it. His family was poor but he'd built himself a raft when he was young. He called them 'cradles of the sea!' I dreamt of sailing a real boat, one with a lower deck, a mainsail and a jib. Then I'd discover new islands, establish a beachhead, mark out new territory and explore to my heart's content with only the constellations for guides. So I started to draw that boat. I put it together on paper instead of paying attention to my lessons. I called it *The Press On*."

"It had a single mast, forward on the deck, with only a single mainsail and a jibsail if needed. This type of rigging is very efficient for bay sailing, partly because it moves through air without causing any turbulence. I could maneuver it alone and "tack" closer to the angle of a true wind. It was only about sixteen feet from stem to stern, rather a short allover length for the boats of that time. Her beam wide, her cockpit huge, she would contain all that I needed in room and make a fine vessel. My plans for my new boat occupied my mind continually, and even my dreams, so that I simply forgot all about the angels."

"One night in late summer I was dreaming of sailing in the Sound. I heard a whirling sound and there they were."

"'Little sailor, we greet thee,' Barak said joyously. 'Thy boat is lovely to behold. May we sail with thee?'"

"What could I do but welcome them? They were so bright that as we stood together on deck the darkness lifted until it seemed almost like daylight! Silas read my thoughts. 'The brightness of angels is due to their purity of spirit. Since there is no darkness in Heaven, he said, I musn't be concerned if they lit up everything around them when they came to earth, even if it was to visit my dream. *For God, who commanded the light to shine out of darkness, hath shined in our hearts, to give the light of the knowledge of the glory of God in the face of Jesus Christ.* Silas fixed his eyes on a star above us, a white forefinger pointing toward Heaven. Barak solemnly watched, lips pursed in thought."

"In a voice like the wind Silas spoke first, his arm still raised toward the stars."

"'The moon tonight is at its highest arc and the hour grows late. Art thou in readiness?'"

A notebook and pencil appeared before me on a table. We bowed our heads and Barak offered up a prayer to Heavenly Father that was as long as Silas' had been. I remember how sweet it was. He gave thanks for all *my* blessings, praised the Lord and the Holy Ghost, 'the purveyor of all truth and light as it emanates from the highest perfection of our Lord Jesus Christ.'

Part Three: Latitudes

Nine

"'The lesson tonight is about God's love for His creatures here on earth. What dost thou know of love, my sweet Marshall?'"

"I pondered that for awhile. I thought about all the things that gave me pleasure, and than said 'I love to sail. Love to fish, love trains and boats and pirates, and...' But they were frowning."

"Silas said slowly 'That's 'pleasure' you speak of. But the love of God is greater and brings with it, joy. God is thy eternal Father. He is the supreme Ruler of Heaven and earth and all that has been, that now is, and that will ever be. Who made the fish thou loves to catch, Marshall? Who gave men their able minds and nimble hands that they could build those boats, and who supplied the forests and trees whence lumber comes? Love is the first and final answer to all questions in life. God has given thee thy body and its breath, Marshall. He knows the hairs upon thy head and his angels whisper to thee that all is well when thou sleeps."

"'God, our Father, is a merciful man. He *is* love, he is gentleness and mercy and he wants so much to forgive us when we ask. Once thou realizes the love that Father God and thy brother Jesus Christ have for thee, thou will never fail to believe that eternal life is within thy grasp. We angels come to all of God's children to give the message to their hearts and they receive these messages, each in their own spirit. Then their sleep is full of rosy dreams and they think thoughts of peace and contentment. We shower care upon them and we have great love for thee, our brave sailor.'

"Barak nodded enthusiastically and chuckled. 'Yes, yes, we bring peace to all creatures through the agency of the Father. We love to love, you know!'"

"I was writing in my book as fast as I could, but it was a tough subject to grasp."

"'Marshall, put down thy pen. Close thy dream eyes and think for a moment upon the great problem that faced a father. A father that might have been thy own, or which might one day be thee, but for time and circumstance. Dost thou remember the story of Abraham and Isaac?'

"Oh, that old story, about Abraham being told to sacrifice his son to God. I remembered it, all right, and I was real glad I wasn't in Isaac's position."

"'Perhaps thou missed the great significance of that story, my sweet charge.' Barak took the lead in this instance. 'What do we remember of Father Abraham? He was an old man when Isaac was born. He was also rich but did not set his heart upon the things of this world. Remember that our Lord favored him, calling him to leave his homeland and to wander? Dost thou think he was an adventurer?'"

"I didn't remember that Abraham *liked* to travel, especially in that hot desert country. I knew of his love for his wife and children, and I knew that he was one of the early prophets of God, but he didn't live for adventure, as I seemed to do."

"Barak continued. 'Marshall, there are adventures for the body and there are adventures of the spirit. Now Abraham was a righteous man who loved the words of God. We knew him. He was beloved of the Lord who came to Abram when he was ninety-nine years old and had proven himself worthy before his Maker. At that time God commanded Abram to be perfect and made with him a holy promise that as *Abraham* he would become father of many nations in two specific ways. One involved his having children and the other concerned all who would become true followers of Christ.'"

"Silas took over, nodding solemnly. 'Yes, I recall one of our many talks with the great patriarch. He cried in joy when the Lord spoke to him. Oh, he was not without minor faults, but he strove continually to be worthy of the Lord's blessings. That is why, when Isaac was thought to be the sacrifice, Father Abraham was faced with the greatest possible test of his faith. Dost thou remember what happened, Marshall?'"

Marshall put his journal down. He stood up to stretch, and walked around his office a bit, leaning on his cane.

"I, of course, had not studied my lessons, so I knew little of the trials of Abraham, but I did recall that at the crucial moment when Isaac was bound and Abraham had raised his killing knife, God called out to Abraham and told him Isaac was not the sacrifice. I was really relieved when I read that part!"

"Silas continued in his deep throated monotone. He must have been as tall as seven feet, but lightweight, so that when he moved it seemed he did so all at once, not as regular people do, one foot at a time to stay balanced. He and Barak sort of floated, as if on the air and ground at the same time. After I got used to it, I tried to move in the same way, but it ended in a jump. Barak got a good laugh from that one."

"'Little navigator, we wish thee to know that thy Father in Heaven cares for thee above all who will ever love thee. He promises thee eternal life with Him in return for thy faith and thy obedience to His teachings. Now, Abraham did not hesitate to follow the commandment to sacrifice Isaac, who had complete trust in God and in his father. He was spared death as reward for his deep faith and for *his* father's enduring, unquestioning trust. We were at that great occasion when our Lord Jehovah called out to Abraham to stay his hand. It was a magnificent moment in the spiritual progression of this planet!'"

Barak said "Modern prophets are no different. We are here to tell thee that thou must pay attention to the teachings of the great men of thy time, the leaders of thy Church, for in their words are the words of salvation. Remember, it is through faith in the Gospel that we find the joy in life.'"

"'Silas spread his arms across the deck of the ship, no doubt reliving that great emotional moment. Barak had taken to walking back and forth, his head bobbing up and down in punctuation of Silas' speech. 'Yes, yes. That is *true* adventure. Now, had Abraham put his own will before the will of the Lord on that occasion and not agreed to do as he was commanded, he would not have known the infinite mercy of God.'"

"'We, as angels of the Lord, know that *thy* father and mother at home love thee with all their heart and would gladly give their lives to save thy own if required. Thy heavenly Creator cares about thee most of all. Our point is that when thou lives as Christ wishes thee to and honors thy parents, thy blessings will be numerous and thy problems will melt away.'

"Silas's deep voice trembled. His white arms moved slowly upward as he spoke and, as if lifting some great gift up to God for His approval, hung in the air. Barak was nodding from side to side. He wiped teary eyes with the edge of his gown. Like opposite ends of the same thought, they looked toward the heavens in reverence, a pair of glistening holy angels of God. We were all silent as the significance of that moment in history passed again before them and penetrated forever the fabric of my own heart. I have never been more aware of my childish ignorance in the face of such perfect understanding than at that moment."

Hearing their words, I felt terrible. Where was my faith, my trust? How would God test me? No, I corrected myself, God is already testing me, and I am probably the biggest failure He has ever known. I must be very disappointing to Heavenly Father. How many times had I disobeyed my parents, my bishop and my teachers? I had never repented of anything! I rolled the bottom of my shirt between my fingers. What kind of an Isaac would I have been? Was it too late to repent? Would He listen? I fell to my knees before the angels. They spread their white arms over me and bowed their heads with me.

"I'm sorry, Father," my heart said. "I am so very sorry. I've been so blind. I pray you will forgive me the dumb things I've done."

"Suddenly, a melody broke over our heads, I heard it clearly. It was soft but very strong. I'd never heard heavenly choirs before, but Barak began to smile, and then his smile became laughter. Silas, who'd been standing there kind of transfixed, slowly folded his arms into a praying position. The music became louder. I heard their wonderful voices singing. Silas and Barak knew the words and sang them. Barak said 'It's the heavenly choir! Isn't that wonderful? Hearken!'"

The prophets of God help each of us to find the way, the music seemed to say, *as they lovingly instruct and guide us back to His presence, just as our Heavenly Father showers us with His perfect love and care.*

"I craned my neck skyward, tilting my head to catch the soft, fleeting sounds. I can't describe it, the whole sky was alive with song. I tried to make out the words, but only these few came to me..."

Night winds that sweep across thy dreams, blowing dust off the stars, move thee.

Move, thy little craft, in ever-widening circles toward the farthest reaches of sleep. Sail beneath vast branches of stars and turn away thy sister world of dreams until angels are all that encircle thee.

"Then I heard another song:

'I wander through the still of night,
When solitude is everywhere--

65

Alone, beneath the starry light
And yet I know that God is there.

I kneel upon the grass and pray;
An answer comes without a voice.
It takes my burden all away
And makes my aching heart rejoice.'"

"Somewhere inside I felt a lifting of weight from my mind, a new peace. My heart was being changed in those moments. A question came to me, awaiting an answer. *Had they sung to me before and I never heard them until now?* I knew I'd have to find the solutions to many questions before true rest would come."

Ten

Aunt Sylvia, Marshall's adopted daughter came to Ruth's classroom as she was gathering up her summer midterm tests. From experience she knew that when they were returned to her hapless students they'd look bloody from her red penciled attacks and the thought made her smile.

Sylvia was trim and smartly dressed, with a sweet demeanor and a soft smile. She was a handsome woman with a professional attitude toward life. Her brown hair matched her eyes and she seemed content with her state of affairs. Once a teacher in another state, Sylvia happily gave it up in favor of marriage to an architect. She and Ruth sat in schoolroom chairs and chatted about many things before they broached the subject of Marshall Cannon. Sylvia studied her hands a moment before plunging in.

"Marshall is a very special person. I really don't know much about his early life. He served in World War II for awhile. He was decorated for bravery under fire, but he won't talk about it. After the war he became a navigational engineer, you know, with his own business. The northwest and the Territories was his area, you might say. Then he found Naida, an Indian woman from Sitka, Alaska. He married her as soon as she'd let him. He told me they were very much in love. But she died a few years later and he grieved for her many years before he was able to lay it to rest. For a couple of years afterward he was so distraught that he disappeared. None of his family knows where he went. We asked him many times, but he would never tell us."

Ruth asked about Naida. Sylvia shook her head sadly.

"Naida was much younger than Marsh, but they fell in love instantly, according to his own story. She was a quiet woman, not much more than a teenager, really. Naida was a pure spirit, as Marshall told me. There was no guile in her. Her thoughts always seemed to be for others and people showered her with love in return. Marshall met her at a native dance in a small town outside Sitka, where he had gone to meet a business partner. Naida and her mother were at the dance, her mother acted as a chaperone. Marshall spotted her and asked her to dance. He claims that when Naida blushed and looked at him he knew she would become his wife.

"Marshall promptly courted her all over the ice while he taught her the Plan of Salvation. Then he took her all the way to Utah to be baptized. He wanted to marry her then, but she wanted her family around her so they went back to Alaska and he proposed to her again in front of her family. She accepted with a smile and the words 'I will be yours forever.' He's quite the romantic! They were sealed in that lovely temple two years later."

Ruth tried to imagine Marshall as a young man, courting Naida.

"It sounds like him, so positive about life. So how did she die?"

Sylvia walked to the window that looked out upon the hills beyond. She stood for some moments without speaking.

"We don't like to talk about that, but I'll tell you a bit of it, since you are kind of his biographer and the insight will be helpful. Naida was very attached to her family, they were fishermen, so she and Marsh lived near them in one of the small inlets off southwest Alaska. They were hoping for a child. One summer day several years after their marriage, as Marsh told the story to me, Naida wanted to visit a neighbor who lived a half mile away through some forested area. He heard her scream a few minutes after she'd left the house. He ran out to find her confronting a black bear that had wandered close to their home. Bears are common up there and through our upstairs windows we could see a family of them grazing. Naida must have inadvertently disturbed their foraging. The female roared and came right for her. She probably attacked to protect her cubs."

"Marsh had grabbed his rifle on his way out the door, but when he reached Naida the bear already had her and came right for him, clawing at his leg. He had to wrestle himself loose. That's where his limp comes from. It took four shots to the head to drop that creature, but it was too late for Naida. When he finally got her to the hospital they eventually discovered she was pregnant. Medicine was not what it is today, you can imagine. Mother and child perished."

68

Sylvia's eyes were full. "You know," she said, "Marsh went to the Lord that very day. He was deeply grieved at his loss, but he was overheard telling his Father in Heaven of his love. I wasn't there, of course, but stories of his great faith are legend in our family. He told the Lord that it was all right that he had taken Naida if God needed her, because he knew they would be together again, and they would raise their child in eternity. Then he went to her family and brought them all to the little branch of the Church in town. They were not LDS, but within a year they all joined. After that he disappeared for several years. Just up and left town, walked away from all his possessions. To my knowledge he has never told anyone where he went. I suppose he just wanted to grieve privately and not bother any of his family with it."

She shrugged and smiled the way people do when they have lived with unanswered questions for a long time.

"But he must have needed solace," Ruth ventured. "Why would he disappear like that?"

Sylvia shook her head. "I have asked him many times, but he just waves his hand at me and says ''Trust, just trust.'"

"Sylvia, if his wife and child were killed, how did you happen along? Did he remarry?"

Sylvia laughed. "No, he never even looked at another woman, but I know that he wanted a child to fill in his terrible loneliness. Some years after Naida's death he met an old woman who told him about Margaret and myself. My sister and I are orphans. We were abandoned at birth. Marsh discovered us in a very ugly situation - I'd rather not discuss that part of my life - and he rescued us. He adopted us and raised us both through some very tough times. We owe our lives to him. He brought me to the Lord and his Church. He's my hero and my dearest friend."

Sylvia took Ruth's hand and pressed it.

"You have been sent as his biographer. Whatever he tells you, treat it with love and care. Marsh has provided for us and our families all these years. We all love him dearly. Be very gentle in telling his story, will you?"

Ruth felt encouraged by Sylvia's devotion to her adopted father. It helped her to understand him. She could not even imagine his grief at losing Naida, and she wondered at the strength he had shown in his determination to teach her family the Gospel. But what could explain his disappearance? Was this the secret he'd been holding back? His inner strength, she knew, must have come of his time with the angels. The principle of adoption works in many ways, she thought. We are born of God, we come to earth, accept Christ as our Savior. Through baptism we are adopted into the Abrahamic Covenant, we seal our dead to ourselves. The links become forged forever and through that chain of love we create an eternal family. What a wondrous Plan the Lord has given us.

She thought of her own feelings. They'd changed considerably for the better since knowing Marshall. He was a thoughtful host, catering to her spirit and her stomach, thanks to Mrs. Willow's cooking. His stories of the angels gladdened her and gave her faith. Sometimes they'd talk late into the night or take walks along the waterfront near his boat landing. Slowly, Ruth began to unburden herself. She told Marshall about her parents' fight and her father's disappearance from their lives.

She shared some of her dreams and frustrations with Marshall, who gave her counsel born of his long life. Ruth began to blossom, to feel a new calmness and strength. But continually the thought nagged at her that he was growing weaker and their time together was running out. She tried to put it out of her mind as she drove the highway to his home for another session. Marshall had told her that his story was nearing the finish but he still had not hinted of the secret he carried.

On Ruth's arrival she found him sitting comfortably with Mrs. Willow in their spacious living room, in good humor. They had been sharing a laugh and she came to the door chuckling.

"Oh, we're so glad you're here today. Marsh was just telling me a new joke he'd heard at church. Do come in and have some cobbler with us."

70

It was easy to feel at home among these two lovely spirits. Ruth thanked her for her kindness and bit into the tastiest early blackberry cobbler possible. Marshall was just finishing his dessert. He shared his joke with Ruth and they laughed. She had become very dear to him. He was grateful that she looked upon him in a fatherly way and he was careful to give her whatever support he could. He thought sadly of the many empty years he'd spent working, his children grown and gone, no family to welcome him home. Those years had toughened him, cleansed his spirit. He had little distraction to his inward thoughts and his loneliness he poured out unto the Lord.

It was from these times he gained his greatest understanding of his own frailty. This child (for he was old enough to be her grandfather) had begun to open her heart to him. He could sense in her the makings of a strong and spiritual woman.

"What have you been up to," he asked, ready to tease about her classroom anxieties.

"I spoke with your daughter, Sylvia, last week, Marshall. She's really glad for the work we are doing here."

"Oh? Was she helpful?"

He didn't seem too interested.

"She was very helpful. She filled me in a little bit on your background. I hope you don't mind?"

He shrugged and pushed his plate aside.

"Sylvia is precious to me, as are all my family. I'm sure she didn't divulge any family secrets. So long as you only write the story *I* tell you, I have no concern. My background is not germane to our work, but what I have to tell you today and during this next month, those are the things to concentrate on, Ruth.

"This story is not about me, really, but about faith in God, about His love for us and how He lets us know He is always on our side."

"I understand that, Marshall. I did enjoy her, though. She thinks your life is full of mystery."

Marshall let out a laugh. He was enjoying this.

"Mystery? Why would she say that?"

71

"She told me about your wife, Naida, and how she was killed. Sylvia says you disappeared after that. None of your relatives know what happened to you. I was wondering, too. May I ask where you --"

Ruth broke off, seeing the look on Marshall's face. He pushed back from the table and stood up. Taking his cane from the back of the chair he moved toward the bay window at the end of the room and stared out at the traveling sea. Ruth and Mrs. Willow exchanged glances. Ruth was instantly sorry, afraid she had again provoked Marshall too far. After all, it was his life and his business and it had little to do with the story of angels that he considered so important.

She was there again, among the swaying branches above the bay. Her hair was long and lustrous black. He would run his fingers through it and find in her eyes a reflection of his own love for her. Never had a woman so moved him as Naida. Only when he found her did his life truly begin. God had sent him to find her, they both knew it. Why had he lost her so soon?

For an instant the moment returned to him, her screams, his running with the rifle he grabbed so fast he didn't remember if he or Naida had reloaded it the day before. He'd had a quick image of himself cracking the rifle butt across the bear's head. He knew they were both doomed if the rifle had only bullet or two left in it. He screamed out

"Save her. Oh, Father, save her!"

Then he was grabbing her, pushing her down and behind him. Blood from her hit him in the face. She was moaning in pain, from deep within her she gasped for life, rolling away from the beast that had reared up. In a second he turned around for another attack. Marshall hated himself for trembling as he raised the rifle to his eyes. Quickly he squeezed off a shot. It hit the bear near his left cheek and glanced off. He roared in pain and raised himself to his full height, taller than Marshall, pawing the air. But the shot had stopped his advance.

Marshall's thoughts raced. He had to aim truly now and finish it. He cocked the gun as the bear came toward him. He shot again, not knowing how many bullets were left. Naida was screaming. The second bullet hit the bear in the shoulder. He

72

danced backward and roared in pain. Quickly Marshall aimed again higher and shot off twice more, scoring in the bear's neck and head. That did it. With a lurch the bear wheeled backward, writhing in agony. He fell to the earth and lay there, finally still. His blood was everywhere, thicker and darker than the woman's. Marshall was covered with the blood of them both.

He threw the rifle down and turned to find Naida. She no longer cried out, her arms were gripped around herself. She wasn't breathing. He yelled to her, again and again, calling her back to him, but he feared she was gone. No one was near to call for help. He picked her up. Then it was his own sobs he heard, his own heart that was breaking, his life that longed to follow her past this tragedy. That is what he remembered of her last moments with him.

But he did not run away from his grief. His leaving was given to him as a healing, a way to make peace with pain and to deepen his understanding. The angels had taught him well, and that day they came to him in answer to his cries. They ministered to him and sent him forth. He had never told anyone where or why. Those few years following Naida's death began as a trial of faith and endurance, but they became for him a touchstone that he might endure living with only the Lord for his comfort. No one else could understand that as he could, not even Ruth. That is why the past had to belong to him alone, at least for now. Now he had another task, and very little time.

Marshall turned to face the women at the table. He was sorry he couldn't share it with them. They would have to accept that. He hobbled over and smiled tiredly to relieve some of the anxiety he saw in their faces.

"It's all right, I'm all right. No, I can't share that with you at this time. I know that you're curious. I'm sorry."

"I'm sorry, too," Ruth said. She felt an inch tall.

Marshall turned on his cane to head down the hallway to his office.

"Let's get to work," he said. "Lots to do, not much more time."

Then he smiled at them both and shrugged.

Part Four: Dead Reckoning

Eleven

"Marshall, little one of light
Whom the angels dote upon,
Grow up to be like your Father in Heaven
And inherit all He has.
He loves thee, thou sweet child.
He wept for thy beauty as He made thee...
God fosters His undying love and devotion to thee.
His angels will teach thee.
And thou will come to us in happiness and light.
And now, little traveler, sweet dreams, good night.''

77

Notes: August 22nd

"My lessons were never planned, but I was taught well. One time they would teach me about repentance, another night it would be the role of prophets in our lives. Yet another time would be concerned totally with the love of the Father for His children or the role of the Savior. They became my friends, Ruth, citizens of my dreams. They told me their home was in my heart. Imagine that, in my heart!"

"I never knew when they'd show up. They simply came to call when they decided I needed to be enlightened, which was often. I remember one night we were discussing navigation.

"'Thou would be a navigator. It is urgently important that thou understand thy relationship to thy craft, which has a covering of skin across stays and ribs like unto thine own body. As thy boat awaits thy inhabiting, thou art a craft upon the waters of life, hewn and sewn by thy Father who has put into thee His spirit and Who waits upon thee in His heaven. When thou are housed within thy boat upon the water thou are at the mercy of the current, both the set and drift. In thy attempts to sail a straight line to thy Father's kingdom of love and righteousness, currents create forces that by their nature will move thy little boat from its charted position to a different one. In this way the set of thy journey may be thwarted. Thou will observe by watching the sea that this change of course is due to the current's drift in concert with the velocity of the tide that carries it. Dost thou see the comparison clearly?'"

"Barak greatly enjoyed these conversations. I considered his statements, keeping in mind the metaphor of myself with the sea. 'But the rudder will correct for set and drift. That way I can straighten out again. Then, Barak, there's the compass.'"

"'"It is thy hands which move the rudder and the oars, Marshall, and thy heart which moves thy hands. I say unto you, can ye look up to God at that day with a pure heart and clean hands? I say unto you, can you look up, having the image of God engraven upon your countenances? Without correct and eternal principles engraven upon thy heart of hearts thy boat will stray into waters which will carry thee to the Adversary, who awaits thee with his legions in the waters of thy mortal life, compass or no.'"

"I thought about that a long time, remembering my father's caution about straying away from the compass' bearings when sailing on the Sound. He told me that as long as I knew where the shoreline was (and in which direction I was sailing) I could find my way back home. In time I discovered more than that. I found out that the true shoreline of a life is the word of the Lord.

"Silas took up the conversation. 'That is dead reckoning, a useful tool when all other means of navigation fail. But, when in the fog of confusion that ties upon the water as upon the mind, a new plotting must be taken every few minutes to prevent straying and to assure that the rod of correct direction not be lost. The shore is a landmark, and there are more. The scriptures are our books of instruction in this life and in all others. Referring to them often is the only way to sail a direct line to the Father's waiting arms.'"

"'Don't forget the Church and the temples,' Barak added with happy emphasis. 'Where would the Saints be without their endowments and work for their dead?'"

"'Correct, dear companion,' said Silas. 'Our Lord cherishes each of us and he brings to us his mind and will. In this way his children can receive his revelation for their lives at any time, for our Holy Ghost never sleeps but lives to impart holy instruction to the minds and hearts of all children of the Lord. In this way we can always be safe from the proximity of danger.'"

"While I was contemplating the relationship between revelation and my compass, suddenly, like an object lesson, a light formed itself before my eyes, opening upon a vast whiteness in which I beheld a strange vision. It seemed to consist of a rolling ball of yellow matter, but as I watched I discerned within the brightness four objects, like small obelisks. These remained stationary, and they reminded me of compass settings, filled with intense light and located at points to the east and west, north and south of the circle. These heavier 'markers seemed to pulse with their own light. I blinked, thinking I was hallucinating, but then I heard laughter. Before I could turn around, four small angelic spirits came into my sight and took their positions within the brilliance of the circle, which now appeared like ribbons of white fire. Each figure stationed itself at one of the four points and hovered in the light."

"My impression was that they guarded our Father's merciful gift to mankind, the choosing of a life's path. There they rested, as if to become fixed upon these essential poles of light, and they sang out to me a sweeter melody than I have ever heard. Very little of it has stayed in my memory, but I recall that the cherub at the point of highest elevation sang with the most fervor:

'The Compass of Eternal Life
Make it a bracelet around thy heart.
Let it sing to thy soul where 'ere thou roam.
True north is where all bearings start, the mariner's star.
With grateful labor choose thy scope and grasp the wheel
0 Wanderer, find the Word and bear thee Home.'

"I just stood there transfixed at this immense display before me. Have we ever thought how important our life choices are to a loving Father in Heaven? But a few moments later, the vision seemed to withdraw, the lights grew dimmer as the music ceased and a warm wind gently poured past my ears. Rubbing my eyes didn't help, for the darkness of the deck quickly returned and I found myself staring into a starry night, calm and natural, with only my amazement for company! I can't even be sure I really dreamed it. The strangest thing, it was..."

Marshall looked up from his reading. His eyes were reddened and he looked very tired. Just thinking about all that lay ahead to record was a great strain upon him, but he knew the meat of his story was very near.

"I'll always remember that discussion. It taught me so much. It saved me from turmoil later in my life as a navigator. My, I was so fortunate to know those angels. Many times they spoke to me of the heavens we take for granted. I remember one night, Barak and Silas were on deck, stargazing our galaxy."

"'There is Ankaa, part of the Phoenix,' Barak began. 'The ancients loved this constellation. They saw in it a symbol of renewal and immortality. And there - Praesepe in Cancer, Trapezium in Orion! How like a beehive of activity.'"

"'Oh, they are sublime, thou Barak, yes, but took here at the lovely Pleiades' cluster of beauties. Who on earth can know of their richness and their perfection of light? See, there, that one is bluish-white, another is red, a third is yellow. We were there for the forming of Aldebaran, dost thou remember?'"

"Barak was deep in reverie. 'We heralded so many stars in the universes of the Father. Their magnitudes, their luminosity. Algol, for example, and the breathtaking Betelgeuse. Because the Father placed them perfectly, astronomers and navigators throughout time have depended for their lives upon them. Remember the new star that guided the prophets to the Christ child? How magnificent the Plan of our Father in Heaven. Praised be His name.'"

And I, God, made two great lights; the greater light to rule the day, and the lesser light to rule the night, and the greater light was the sun, and the lesser light was the moon, and the stars also were made even according to my word. And I, God, set them in the firmament of the heaven to give light upon the earth.

"That night we sailed beneath the stars. Clusters and constellations whirled and sang praises to God. Barak called it "a congress of stars." He talked about their earthly symbolism, saying that men give their meaning to things that God makes, not thinking to ask God what purpose they serve. Like a dope, I said it might be interesting to rearrange the heavens. Silas gave me a withering look and shook his finger."

"'Marshall, thou youngest one, rearrange thy thinking. The Father hath set these lights upon eternal paths. All things bear an intelligence which allows them to function perfectly within their given sphere of existence. Each of God's creations hearken to Him and to the Lord of Hosts. They perfectly obey the commands of God Who sets them into motion. Each orbit of every celestial body is set, its pathway perfectly reckoned for the slightest degree of motion, calculated to be in concert with every other.'"

81

Each star perfectly obeys its orbit; each unfolds its potential in the time of the Lord, for the good and perfection of all things. Our Lord's house is a house of order. The lights of heaven may not vary in their paths without the word of the Lord who controls the elements. They and all things, as we have told thee, live to obey Father in perfect humility according to the laws He has made. Anyone who thinks that God does not micro-manage each life He sets in motion has much to learn of Heaven. Let me quote our Master:

In the beginning God created the heaven and the earth... The light which is in all things, which giveth life to all things, which is the law by which all things are governed, even the power of God who sitteth upon his throne, who is in the bosom of eternity, who is in the midst of all things... And again, verily I say unto you, he hath given a law unto all things, by which they move in their times and their seasons; and their courses are fixed, even the courses of the heavens and the earth, which comprehend the earth and all the planets.

"I blushed, very aware of my thoughtlessness at taking the wrong tack. I quickly changed the subject."

'What about God's love for all of us?' I hoped this would make them forget my silly request. They did, and this led to a wonderful discussion on truth."

Twelve

"Silas began our discussion by instructing me to take notes so his words would impress themselves permanently upon my mind. This I did and when I awoke I wrote them in this journal."

"Truth is the essence of the universe. It is everywhere at once and bespeaks the perfection of God. It comes on the heels of all that is right in the universe, and God speaks His truth to His angels and His prophets in all its glory. Truth cannot be subsidized by anything less. It admits no error, it is all-encompassing, perfection, the foundation of all true gospel, all that is worthy and light."

"'Darkness comes from the lack of knowing true principles. The Prince of Darkness is very much alive and he and his angels are always at work trying to obstruct the justice of heaven. He does much damage because he is the master of lies and can make them seem to be truths. We see a lot of that here and we fight it daily within the minds of those we serve, such as yourself.'"

"Barak was walking around the boat as it sailed on. While Silas spoke Barak nodded his head affirmatively, shooting out sparks of lightening as he did so. I could tell it was difficult for him to contain his own revelations."

"'Jesus Christ came to tell us the truth. Many listened to him and knew he was a prophet, a holy man. We angels understand him and our perfection is assured because we follow him. Never let truth go or be supplanted by anything else. It is imperishable. It is the living essence of the Lord of light. Truth must be used to better mankind and all that is in the world for good. It never changes and is totally dependable, and that is why Christ is the same today, tomorrow and forever. Evil, of course, is the abdication of truth, disregard for what is real.'"

"They were going so fast, I had trouble keeping up. In my journal, here, I have writing in all the margins and comers of the pages. That talk gave me enough understanding of what the Gospel is about to accomplish many things in later life. What do you think of it?"

Ruth was listening so intently she forgot to notice the tape had played itself through.

"We'll have to record those last sentences again, I'm afraid. I got so involved in their discussion, I forgot... Oh, Marshall, yes, I know those words are true, I know it. How can anyone deny what God tells us is true? You were blessed to have that knowledge given to you. She grabbed a tissue from her purse and blew her nose, very moved by what she'd heard."

"If only the world could hear that, surely they'd --."

"The world has heard it, but I don't think they want to take the responsibility for living it." Marshall turned a page of his journal.

"Listen to this," he said. "The truth will truly set us free. When an individual knows what is true against what is false, that individual reaps the benefits of heaven and is open to the goals which holy angels set before us to achieve. We can achieve miracles of faith when we know how. Then our course becomes set upon the right path which God intended us to have for our lives. Therein lies freedom and truth. Thou, Marshall, are the product of truth."

"Silas again took over. 'I have written a poem about truth, dear child. Dost thou wish to hear it?'"

He was really eager to tell me. Barak urged him on, so what could I do?

'Truth burns in every soul. It burrows in the sea
Until mountains rise to meet the skies.
It shouts from the tops of mountains!
Truth is everyone's pleasure and birthright, the
    foundation of every soul.
Error corrupts, whereas truth builds and edifies.
Thou should embrace truth wherever it is found.
Thou must confound error lest it spread
Like the deadly virus it is.
Come to us and learn the truth for all time!'

"Oh, how happy my angels were with that poem! They danced on the deck and sang for joy. I really wish my parents

84

could have been in that dream with me... I don't know why, but I never did tell them. Never told anyone, but now..."

"Did you ever question the purpose of angels?" Ruth was still hoping that a couple of them would find her.

"No, not really," Marshall answered. "Because they came to me suddenly and told me that I needed them. After a couple of months I realized they were right. But I did question the purpose of the Holy Ghost. Silas would always point to revelation when I did that."

"'It is so important to receive revelation. The third member of the Godhead gives us inspiration so we can be of one mind with Father, and therein lies real maturity of spirit. How can we know what God wants of us, even what we in the premortal existence chose for ourselves, without the reminders which God's angels bring us? Remember thy prophet Alma's questions to those in Zarahemla?'"

'Have ye spiritually been born of God? Have ye received his image in your countenances? Have ye experienced this mighty change in your hearts?'

'Alma was reborn spiritually, as we know. He courageously repented of his sins after he was met by one of our kind and chastised for his damnable behavior. Father in Heaven knew of the goodness and beauty of Alma's soul. He wanted this young man redeemed that he might become a mighty force in the true Church of Christ.'

Silas squeezed shut his eyes. His arms were before him, hands spread.

'Oh, how we all grieved for Alma and his rebellious spirit. He went through an anguishing repentance. We rushed to minister to him, to comfort him in his severest of trials.' Here he stopped, overcome. Barak took over for him with eyes flashing.

"'My, yes, we were at his side the whole time. How he wept and cried out. But he was given to see the miracles that are in store for those who truly believe, and he became a great inspiration to others in time. He was born again in God, truly free, truly at peace. Isn't that a wonderful story?'"

He smiled with gusto and clapped his white hands as his gown danced in the night breeze.

"Why was it so hard for Alma to change," I wondered, but I knew the answer as I spoke the question, for Alma had been a willful man.

"If God had waited, wouldn't Alma have figured it all out eventually?"

"Barak touched my thin shoulders. His voice was soft, and his usually mirthful eyes were filled with love. They twinkled from someplace within him and I saw that he really was a beautiful angel."

"'Marshall, our earnest young sailor, love is at the center of the universe. The compassion and brotherhood that we feel for each other comes from our Father in Heaven. It sustains us all and lets the human soul expand. Then miracles do happen. All the while Alma was destroying the Church of Christ the love of the Father accompanied him on his journey. Alma did not know that. He thought he was destroying evil when he fought against the faithful. His mind and heart was so set upon that destruction that, if left unmet, he would have lost his promise of eternal life and made for himself a house of sin from which he might never exit.'"

Our angels confronted him and bade him listen to the song of care and compassion our Father sings to every soul, and when the dear brave prophet felt the magnificent power of love that God and Christ have for him and for all of creation, he overcame his stubbornness and fell upon his face and was lost in the spirit.'"

Marshall closed his journal and sat back, thinking about his dreams with the angels.

"That was a powerful sermon. It took a lot of them, and you know, the angels taught me so lovingly that slowly but very surely they made this surly boy turn about and pursue a safe path. Oh, I didn't go down in defeat easily. I debated, I denied, I ignored their advice. In every session I argued my points with simple and worldly logic. But they used only loving persuasion and scripture. They said all laws of God are based upon a dual principle:

'Wherefore I give unto them a commandment... Thou shalt love the Lord thy God with all thy heart, with all thy might. Come to us and learn the truth for all time!'

"Oh, how happy my angels were with that poem! They danced on the deck and sang for joy. I really wish my parents could have been in that dream with me... I don't know why, but I never did tell them. Never told anyone, but now..."

"I guess I have to learn what it feels like," I said thoughtfully, thinking that I would hate to miss something as wonderful as all that."

"I, too, love the words of truth," Ruth murmured. "But that commandment is sure hard to follow. Just think, we're brothers and sisters, not enemies, not strangers. If we cared for each other with real intent, there'd be no war, no contention, no power grabbing anywhere in the world."

"True enough, matey. All we have to do is realize the Gospel's divine justice. It's perfect, unlike human laws. Humans can't become perfected while they're mortal, but we can have a perfect moment, a perfect thought, perfect service. When we are performing sacred ordinances then we are being perfect in those acts. Eventually I asked the obvious question."

"What about angels? Are they perfect?"

"Barak and Silas turned to look at me. Then they looked at each other. They'd never been asked that question, I'm sure, by the surprise on their faces. Silas spoke."

"'Even angels have agency, the power to decide for themselves. There have been perhaps a few who have strayed. They are not the subjects of this discussion, Marshall.'"

He pointed a long white finger at my neck and leaned toward me.

"'Thou are the student tonight. Let us continue in earnest while the night is still young?'"

"We talked on for hours. Eventually I had to concede every point to them. Let me tell you, perfection is really hard to argue with! That night I learned much more from my losses than my victories, I can tell you that."

He laughed and Ruth nodded.

"I know about love because of what I feel for my parents, and my friends, and I do love my Father in Heaven very much. But how are we to really understand love on an eternal level, like they do?"

"Reading and pondering on it, I guess," Marshall replied. "That's what I do, read and question and ponder. Look around you, at the things you see, the perfection of a rose, the way things in nature are constructed. Ponder the sunsets as I have done hundreds of times from the bow of a ship. Think, too, of the element of water, how it saves and nourishes, also how it can so quickly destroy us. But God's love is unchanging. It always surrounds each one of us."

Marshall opened his journal and read again from his notes.

"The care that our Heavenly Father has for all His creatures endures forever, Marshall, tougher than any earthly metal. For the charity of God is like an engine pulling the trains of existence along, giving them the spiritual coal and fire that is the heart's food. It burns forever in the human soul. When we feel that way toward someone, love becomes the fruit of our existence, sweet and happy, profoundly satisfying. Have you considered that the ability to care deeply for another is God's greatest gift to this planet?"...

"He had me there. It was a new thought, one that I would ponder often."

"Then why is there so much killing, so much evil in this world?"

"'Men have their agency. That freedom is also given them by the Father and by the Savior. But many use it unwisely. Sadly, they are so intent upon their worldly ways they do not hear our voices in their ears, but only the seduction of the Adversary can reach them. He is very clever and he has known them in premortal times. The feelings of men are not news to the Father of Lies, but we do not speak of him.'

"It all seemed so clear to me, then. To follow God is to follow good. Anything else led eventually to destruction. Why couldn't the world understand such a simple rule?"

"Barak answered my thoughts with a laugh and he patted my shoulder with his pure white hand. It felt very much alive."

"'That is what we angels spend a lot of time questioning, my dear Marshall. 'But the world is distracted by the things they have created. Our voices are heard only by those who seek the joy of knowing their true beginnings.'"

He added that life eternal is having the joy of eternal promise with us always.

'It is the reason for the Savior's existence, you know, and God the Father every day renews his commitment to each of us. For example, thy great affection for thy parents is evidence of the heart's ability to feel that marvelous enjoyment in being a part of another's life.'

"Then love is the answer, I said back to them. 'I do love you both, and it feels good to me.'

"We all laughed at this remark, and from a long way off a voice came to me on the wind. *Love is that special reaching out of soul to soul and spirit to spirit. It unites us all the way we are meant to be connected. I, your Savior, taught many of the love of the Father but few understood. Now I teach it in my Church and through my missionaries, prompting them to use their love in ways that will glorify the name of God in heaven. All that is done in my behalf is done in the name of love. Amen.*"'

Thirteen

"Well, the next day I awoke in a buoyant mood. Would you believe it was a full day before I realized that Jesus Christ had spoken to me in a dream?"

"All that teaching must have changed your behavior. Did you change your ways and stop running off?"

"I did change a lot, though it took time. My parents saw the difference in me. They even asked if I was sick, if I was worried about something. Since I never told them about the angels, they eventually assumed that I'd put my adventurous life behind me, so they let it go at that. We spent more time together as a family, and I felt more at ease with them, but I think I was waiting for something to happen. When that uneasy feeling, the desire to get moving, called me away, I knew I still wasn't free.

"I spent a lot of time drawing my beautiful boat *The Press On*. My mother was always on the lookout for any talent I might have grown during the night. She bought paper, pens, that stuff, and I started filling up sketch pads with pictures of my beauty, coming about or unfurled before the wind."

"My father really liked my drawings of *The Press On*. He was raised near Vancouver Island off the North Pacific coastline. Fished alongside his father. He set nets for Dungeness crab. His mother cooked all he could harvest. We used to talk about the hazards of sailing the straits of the northwest's puzzle-piece islands."

"He said the sink of the greater Sound extends six hundred feet downward in many places, about ten fathoms, and it's constantly changing because of the uneven land beneath it. The water can become thrashing and unpredictable when a change in current disturbs its flow. It pitches and tosses like some kind of animal. That's the time to stay on land, because the sea is a separate body with many moods. I'd always thought of the ocean as a friend but I found it could just as easily become my enemy. It doesn't know we are there, and it doesn't care. It's a tempest. My father said that everyone who rides the sea carries a silent prayer for mercy packed up and stowed within, just in case, because no one can trust it."

Marshall reached over and picked up the model of the canoe.

"I proved him right. I've sailed the world's oceans for many a year and I known its ruthless power. But I also never forgot that Jesus stilled the waters and walked upon them. Who since then has had his faith? No, men are no match for the sea."

Ruth hurried home after the interview. There were many things to get ready before her classes the next morning. But her thoughts of duty were constantly interrupted by the things Marshall had shared with her. Though it would all be given away to his family, Ruth was the first grateful recipient of these marvelous insights and they were bringing to her mind memories from her own youth. She hadn't realized that the love she carried for her father even now was a gift from God. Her mother's care and sweetness with her came from the Savior's forgiving compassion.

"How simple it really is. But the world keeps us from understanding God," she said to the sea around her.

In the quiet of her room the truth of that simple promise came into her heart, as it came to Marshall so long ago while he toiled in his heart to push it away, desiring only to remain unrepentant and set upon his own pleasures.

Have I fixed my course according to the will of God, she wondered? Ruth thought of her life, its sameness, its spirit-dulling routines, grown up around her like weeds. Suddenly the answer was clear. She needed more faith in Christ, greater love for him. For the first time in years Ruth asked herself what it would take to achieve that, then laughed at the enormity of the question. She thought of Marshall's passionate love of God, his missionary work and his strong spirit so filled with love for the Lord that it shone as a beacon. Even in his greatest trials he was constant in his faith.

"Your salvation is why you're here," Marshall had told her. "Seek it with the same passion and diligence of an explorer pursuing his goal."

Fourteen

The new resolve was with Ruth as she made her way to Marshall's home the following week. Summer school had ended and her time could now be dedicated to transcription of the tapes of the interviews and the arranging of notes in an orderly fashion, tasks that occupied many hours and kept her from enjoying several weeks of rest and relaxation. She was moved by a new desire to complete her work, so she gave up the thought of spending time on the beach and doggedly kept on.

Summer was giving way to fall. Crispness invaded the mornings otherwise balmy and lazy. Wild blackberry bushes boasted their large, juicy fruit in response to a hot summer. It was noon and cloudless. The Sound was a white mirror, hot and shining with reflected sun, blocking any view of the water. Even sunglasses failed to dispel the intense glare. Traffic was heavy and Ruth found herself driving with an urgency she didn't understand. Mrs. Willow hailed her from the garden on her arrival, but her welcoming smile was tinted with worry.

"He's in bed, today, dear. You'll have to visit with him there. The missionaries have just gone. He's sitting up, waiting for you."

Ruth felt an edge of fear. "Why is he in bed? Is he ill?" Why hadn't she been called?

Mrs. Willow paused amidst her nasturtiums and turned, shielding her eyes from the insistent sun.

"Didn't you know? He had an attack the other day. He has heart trouble, you know that, and lung problems, too. He's an old man, my dear cousin is, maybe not long for this world."

She said this in a matter-of-fact voice, like she had been telling herself she had to expect the worst, but tears at the comers of her gray eyes gave her away.

"You'll have to knock on his bedroom door and shout out who you are. Marsh's family will be arriving today. Sylvia was to call you, but I guess she..."

Her voice trailed as Ruth hurried into the house.

This was Ruth's first time for trouble like this, but she knew it had to come. Their last session had left him weak and tired. She prayed as she hurried down the hallway. Please, God, not now, not yet, I don't want to lose him. Ruth knocked at Marshall's bedroom door, yelling her name through it. He called for her to come in, and with a smile that fooled no one, Ruth opened the door. He lay propped upon his pillow, an altered man. In his nostrils tubes bringing his sick body oxygen wheezed slowly.

He looked exhausted of life. The sparkle and energy Ruth had grown accustomed to was gone, so much that she almost didn't recognize him. It hit her with a punch to the stomach.

"It's my ticker," he said weakly, smiling a little. "The old clock's winding down."

The right side of his mouth was droopy. His left arm and hand were slack, propped on a bed tray that held a small glass of juice and several white pills. Was he also mentally incapacitated? Ruth fought the tears back, but Marshall recognized her and reached out slowly with his right arm. He motioned her to him with a one-sided smile. It was only when Ruth looked into his eyes that she recognized his spirit was intact. Hoarsely, he said

"How are you, my friend? Long time, no see."

Seeing the look on Ruth's face, Marshall reached out for her wrist. His eyes were bright with fever but his voice was still firm. She sat on the bed and watched him. Slowly he spoke, his voice hoarse.

"Look here, we're going to finish this story, all right? I'm not dying until I've told you the whole thing. Are you ready to hear it?"

Ruth swallowed hard but she saw his determination was strong as ever.

"I'm ready to go all the way with it, Marshall, however long it takes."

Those were the words he wanted to hear. He patted her hand.

"Go get your tape recorder," he whispered. "Will you bring me my journal?"

Ruth set up the recorder near the bed and fetched the journal from across the hall. She moved slowly, unsure of her movements, still numb with surprise and worry.

"Can I help, Ruth?"

It was Mrs. Willow. Her face, though it wore a smile, was set as if in stone. Ruth wondered where she'd go when Marshall died. She had no surviving relatives her own age, which Ruth estimated to be around eighty. But surely Marshall had provided for her in his will. She went to the older woman and they hugged for a moment.

"We're going to work awhile. Just for awhile. He still wants to go on."

Mrs. Willow turned toward her cousin's room.

"He's a determined old guy,' she said. "I wish he'd just rest 'til he's stronger, but I know him when he sets his mind. Just hurry it up as much as you can. If he gets worn out again..."

She broke off.

"Thank you, I'll be watchful of him, I promise."

They were both near tears. When all had been made ready, Ruth put the microphone close to Marshall's lips and turned the volume all the way up to catch his whispers. With much difficulty, the old man began to read out of the journal.

"This is my favorite part, Ruth. We were talking about dreams. I wondered if angels ever slept or dreamt.

'We do not tire, young one,' I recall Barak telling me. 'But more will be revealed when thy time comes.' He would say no more on the subject, but he quoted his favorite psalm. It's here on this page. I wrote it down."

He showed it to her and Ruth read it aloud into the microphone.

When I consider thy heavens, the work of thy fingers, the moon and the stars, which thou hast ordained - what is man, that thou are mindful of him? And the son of man, that thou visitest him? For thou hast made him a little lower than the angels, and hast crowned him with glory and honour.

"Magnificent, isn't it? One night, after a hard day at school taking exams I came home exhausted. I couldn't even bring myself to play basketball at the hoop outside the barn and I just

97

trudged upstairs to bed. My mother came up with some warm chocolate milk, my favorite, and felt my forehead."

"Are you coming down with a cold, young one? Wait here, I'll get you an aspirin."

But I didn't wait for her. I remember pulling on a knotted shoestring until it broke. I threw the shoe behind me and crawled into bed. In a few minutes I fell asleep.

Fifteen

"I was sleeping soundly when someone called me. It took a few minutes to wake up enough to hear it. I saw a man, average in height and build, his cropped white hair was combed toward his face and ears. This left some baldness on the top of his head, but as he was somewhat aglow, it only made him look more angelic. What really struck me about him was his face. It was the face of youth, of great energy, as if his frame was only a covering to hold the energy within.

"Now I was aware of being in an immense room with an oval ceiling, long as a football field. It also glowed but there was no glare, only a golden softness. The room seemed to be lit from inside the walls, which were curved toward each other, so that it appeared I was standing inside a golden dome. It reminded me of a planetarium I saw once. Everything was yellow and gold. All around this very high-ceilinged room were desks, more than I could easily count. There were machine-like devices. I couldn't figure those out, they looked like today's computers and there was one on each desk. Each device had a huge screen set above several dials."

"The whole area reminded me of work stations. A person, maybe it was a person, dressed in white, sat at each one of these tables. Their fingers moved on a kind of keypad, and when they did that, pictures and text flashed across the screens. There were lists of names, moving across the monitors with such speed it was impossible to see anything but a blur. I estimated there were over five hundred stations in the room, yet nothing was crowded. Everyone was busy and no one spoke. Then I heard choir music from beyond those amber-colored walls. Ruth, it was so perfectly peaceful. I felt like sitting down right there and singing along with the music. It was very moving."

"I looked above my head, but there was no real ceiling. What I thought was a mural turned out to be slowly moving stars. I saw comets whiz past, leaving tails of blue, red and white in their wake. I saw planets, white and a golden starlight, constellations of incredible beauty, glorious and glistering, lighting the room.

Suddenly I remembered I was not there alone. This person was waiting patiently for me to notice him.

"'I am Brother Simon, in charge of this section,' he smiled, eyes twinkling with joyfulness. 'We have been expecting you, Marshall. Your angels-in-charge have brought you to us for this particular session. Won't you let me show you around?'"

"He took my right arm before I could stammer out a comment and we 'walked to a row of work stations. As got closer I saw that the people at the controls looked just like regular men and women, but the men wore white suits, while the women wore white robes that hid their bodies. They were busy with books full of names and they were copying the names into their machines, which seemed to be constructed of a metal I have never in life seen, but .they were real, similar to the computer you're probably working on, Ruth."

Ruth was lost in his story, imagining this new world along with Marshall. She just shook her head and closed her eyes.

"Suddenly I realized that I wasn't anywhere on earth. "Are we in Heaven," I asked? "Am I dead?"

Brother Simon smiled at my outburst.

'Marshall, we do often communicate by thoughts here. The Holy host helps us to transmit our impressions through him to those we wish to receive them, but you have been on earth a long time, and it will take you a while to become used to our culture. No, you are not dead. This is a genealogy center and these folks have been called to do the work for your planet's dead. Of course, they are still living in the spirit. Most of them are here on this planet while they await the Resurrection. When we receive the records from your genealogy workers on earth we input the data here in our machines, which are similar to what you ill be using one hundred years from now.'

"Brother Simon smiled at my shock. We finally stopped before a long row of workstations banking a wall that divided the room lengthwise into halves. These machines were larger and ore complex than the others. I was going to ask what they were for."

"Brother Simon seemed to smile perpetually. He took me by the hand. His own was a little cool to the touch, but an aura of

100

warmth surrounded us. He led me to the back of the largest machine and we walked along the length of the cylinder until we reached a small enclosed space at the junction of two walls. It looked like my parents' closet doors at home. Here Brother Simon pulled back the thick metal door to disclose another door, this one was of wood with a beautiful inlay of gold and other gleaming metals. Its handle was glass, intricately carved and so beautiful that I knew it must lead to some sacred place."

"'This is one of many doors,' Brother Simon informed me.' It goes through to the main rooms. We use the front entrances many yards away for our services. But your enthusiasm is great and your time here very limited, so you will excuse this quick entry, I hope?' I smiled back at him, full of wonderment. We moved through the second door, entering into the largest room I have ever seen. I think it took up a planet!"

"Spread before me across a gleaming ocher marble floor that seemed as wide as the Sound itself was a succession of screens like the giant screens in the theaters of today. There were hundreds of such screens at distances across the auditorium. Moving across them were pictures of live ordinance work as it is carried out in the LDS temples. Many thousands of people were at that moment doing proxy work on earth. I, of course, had no knowledge of it. But my guide explained it all to me while we walked. I could see the baptistries, initiatory rooms and sealing rooms. I counted twelve oxen below each font. Their craftsmanship was perfect, I mean it couldn't be better. It was as if angels had made them. They had such strength and beauty. The fonts were struck in gold. The ceiling was of some intense whitish color and reflected everything that happened. The total effect was one of staggering brilliance. I was overcome with it all, suddenly very dizzy. Brother Simon helped me to sit down. I hit the ground with a thud."

"You haven't taken a breath in some time," he said, laughing.

"Oh, my gosh," I said, groping for breath, groping for words. 'This is, is --"

"Brother Simon, still beside me, nodded quietly."

101

'Heavenly? Yes. It is our central receiving room here in the largest temple on this world. We are below the main floor where thousands of workers come here and take the unending list of names of your planet's dead as they are read into the Lamb's Book of Life and as the proxy work is done on earth. Here we confirm the accuracy and administration of all baptisms, confirmations and sealings that are done here. Whenever a soul's work is being done we find and inform them. Whether or not they accept the work being done for them, they must attend the service to witness it. This is how we keep track of the sacred genealogy that is being done on earth and in heaven to link families forever. It is all done with great speed, order and efficiency, as you might imagine, for we have many billions of worthwhile souls here who desire to accept the Gospel and to be baptized.'

"I was overwhelmed. I must have looked really stupid, just standing there watching the screens. Of course, I didn't understand what was going on and Brother Simon knew it. I asked him what exactly was taking place, but he turned us away from it and told me it was only necessary that I know life can be eternal with God. Then he took me by the shoulders and said with great enthusiasm:

"'How mysterious is God's plan! These souls are mortally dead, yet they live. They have always lived, yet they came to earth with no memory of their past lives. The great adventure of life with body and spirit combined has been theirs. Now they have come back to us in the halls of eternity. Do you see the beauty of it, Marshall?'"

"I remember my amazement. I found a seat and just sat, staring at Brother Simon's illuminated smile. I knew my own life would end, but to see the consequences... It took all my small understanding just to realize I was in a heavenly temple. I know my body's ways, it's rhythms and appetites. It's almost embarrassing, really, to be this way, to live in a body time betrays every day. Yet my spirit is mighty, and one day soon now, it will be free! How I wait for that tirne with joy in my heart! I'm ready for Him, Ruth, ready to go home again."

102

Marshall faltered, his energy waned. Ruth quickly turned off the tape recorder and came to his bedside. She took his hand. It was cold, but he squeezed hers in a solid grip. She couldn't think of what to say. The oxygen pumped steadily away in the quiet room, as if keeping time with his heart. She knew another Plan was operating, not of their earth, but one of eternal scope and perfection. Marshall's life had come along its path, like any traveler on a journey. But here was an intersection, long ago plotted. The turn was marked for him. Probably Barak and Silas were waiting along it, ready to accompany him, talking and laughing along the way to his next destination.

"Let me go on, Ruth. I'm just getting to the exciting part."

"Marshall, please. We can stop for today."

His voice was thin, but he was determined.

"No, just needed to rest. Still more to tell, Ruth. Don't you want to know what happened?"

"Yes, but you're --"

"I'm stubborn. I'm all right, just needed to stop awhile. Let's go on, please."

Ruth sighed and turned the tape recorder back on. Marshall adjusted himself on his pillow and went on in his raspy monotone.

"Brother Simon explained to me that the work I saw was part of what they do in heaven. He said 'As the Saints in temples on earth are doing proxy work, the temples of God in Heaven are brimming with the carrying out in the spirit of those ordinances. We in heaven celebrate those endowments here. I have a surprise for you, if you feel up to it?'

"I was aware that we hadn't spoken out loud during the whole conversation!"

"I followed him. We climbed some steps to the lowest bank of seats nearest a screen and waited for the next group to arrive around us. Soon I heard light laughter. Someone said 'Shush.' I turned to see a large group of temple workers and initiates coming down the aisle toward the screen. With them were two people who looked familiar. The man was sandy-haired and slender. He walked with great energy, almost bounding down the aisle, while the woman behind him followed with a demure step, adjusting her gown. She seemed somewhat older than him and my impression was that they were brother and sister. They were familiar somehow, but I couldn't place them. When they reached the apron near the screen they turned and looked back at me. I think we were sharing the same thought."

"'Marshall? Is that you?' the woman said, then without hesitation she came and took my hand. I was overcome with the sweetness of her spirit. Her face was so known to me. I wanted to say her name, but as I looked at her a painful memory was all that came back. The recollection was dim, but then I saw a picture of a photograph on my dad's dresser. It was an old photo, bent and scarred, barely saved from a fire long ago that had turned the edges and smudged the images of a family. They were my dad's brother and wife, in their forties. It was a typical professional portrait, the parents above the heads of their children. They looked out toward some far off, wonderful destination."

"It was a freak accident. They were all taking a simple weekend trip to the coast to relax and play for a couple of days. John was only about eight. He took his favorite toys and his baby sister Analiese took along her special doll. They started out just after dawn on their trip, hoping to visit some relatives. It was going to be a simple getaway holiday."

"The truck that hit them appeared suddenly. They may not have even seen it until it was too late because of the dense fog along that coast route. They must have had no chance at all of surviving that crash, but the truck driver did all he could to pull them to safety. He did manage to save the woman's purse and a small box of family pictures, but he could do no more. It was a terrible tragedy. My folks grieved for a long time over that and my dad refused to put the picture away. He said they were alive in the spirit and that he wanted us always to remember them as they had been. But to me those faces had become a memorial of death and I couldn't look at them. We never mentioned them without crying."

"'Don't blame God,' my parents told me. 'He took them home and they are happy there. Surely they did not suffer pain of death. We will do their work in the temple when the time comes.'"

But we grieved anyway. They had been our dearest friends and we never really understood why they died. Now these children were again before me, but as adult spirits, with no traces of the terrible tragedy that id taken them. They were gleaming with life and health, full of happy smiles and bouncy energy, as alive as myself. We joyously embraced!

"'Our proxies on earth have just been baptized for us, Marshall. We've just returned to greet you,' Annaliese whispered excitedly. 'In a moment more we return to earth to be sealed to our parents who are waiting for us to join them. Their work is being readied now. Can you stay awhile? We're going to celebrate afterward.'"

With a swift buss on my cheek Annaliese turned and took her brother's hand. The joy of her new adventure radiated throughout me and I shook with happiness. Brother Simon said we could wait a few minutes longer.

"The screen before me showed a man and woman coming forward to take their places in the sealing room. Soon two others joined them. The temple workers beckoned them forward and they knelt at the predetermined places. In a few minutes the ordinance was performed. Now my cousins were joined for eternity with their parents. The family unit had been restored forever and nothing would ever break that bond. Everyone in the room was crying in happiness for these wonderful spirits, including me. I wished with all my heart that my parents could be there to witness this miracle."

"Brother Simon, smiling hugely, said 'These spirits will be returning soon to receive a special blessing. They have invited you to rejoice with them.' He would not answer my inquiries but only said 'Wait and see for yourself. They have planned this with you in mind, Marshall.'"

"Soon the family came into the room holding each other, and all of them were radiant. We all embraced again, and they left to take seats near the screening area to await their blessing. They did not have long to wait. A few minutes passed, minutes as I understood time to be, and then a most wonderful thing occurred.

The door behind us opened quietly, the one Brother Simon and I had entered through, and a man entered the room. Immediately it became still. Conversations ceased. All eyes turned to behold the lucent presence whose face and bearing were that of a man accustomed to a singular rank. The man stood still, letting his gentle but solemn gaze scan the room. Feelings of peace and happiness seemed to emanate from him, and I saw that he gave off a luminous glow of white. I felt that every molecule of life on every universe in that transcending moment beheld his perfection and paid him grateful homage. He was dazzling. Light highlighted his fair hair and shone from his eyes upon everyone there, and all who beheld him were immediately filled with the Holy Ghost, for they began to say 'Praised be the Lord of Hosts! Praised be our Savior.'"

His face was tranquil, yet his countenance was that of a man who had conquered all things. The brightness of his being filled the huge room until its golden walls reflected his radiance. His hair and skin were even whiter than that of my angels. He was neither young nor old, but ageless. His robe was of perfect purity. He wore a second robe, it was the color of crimson, on his right shoulder. He wore it like a cape. I think it signalled the presence of a beloved and much decorated emissary. He stood tall and straight. Justice was in his face and love shone from him and softened the air around him. He was the most beautiful being I have ever seen.

"He saw the family waiting for him, so he approached them. The room was becoming very warm and the .atmosphere heavy. An unmistakable feeling of love seemed to descend like a blanket upon us, which I knew meant it the Holy Ghost was near. Still no one spoke or moved. I know they were caught away in the spirit, because they could only sigh. I felt deep admiration and even love for this man whom I have never (in mortality) seen, and I had an instinctive desire to run up and bow before him, but I held back, waiting for him to speak. He spoke in an even, calm voice, the sure voice of truth and right. It was transmitted to every soul and surely moved every heart."

'My dearest children, I come to thee in the morning of thy new perfection in the kingdom of our Father in Heaven. How I

106

love thee, my dearest ones, and how my Father, who is thy Father, loves thee. His love is of the ages. It flows as balm, as honey from a rock of curtained day, where no one sees the really true marvels of existence. I am that Rock of ages, and from me springs forth eternal life. I am in the Father and He in me. We are one in purpose, in works and in testimony, though we are separate of body and life. Together with the Holy Spirit we make all life available to thee, my blessed children.'

"Annaliese and John were entranced by this man whose infinite gentleness spoke of love and forgiveness. Their parents hugged them. The man in white robes came closer and knelt before them, bidding us all to kneel with them. Then he went on, speaking to them, but to us as well."

"'The love for all our children is the love that springs first from the Father. He it is who wets thy face with a tear, who parts thy lips in smiles and who touches thy cheek in softness and longing for thy return. It is He who is the Author of all things melodious and magnificent. Our Heavenly Father is the Author of love and when we seek love from the heart of another, it is the Father who has taught us that loving kindness is the central meaning of our existence in mortality and immortality. Love for our Father guides our lives and our Father in Heaven's concern for us is the most potent force in the universe. Dost my children love their Father in Heaven?'"

"Analiese and her brother nodded in agreement. They were enthralled. Their parents said they were filled with thankfulness. Then the man arose and spread his arms over the family to bless them. My child's mind received images of the pain he had borne in Gethsemane and of the terrible burden he chose to carry so that none of us would be lost. Through my eyes he still bore the scars of his trials, through my eyes his apostles wept, and his mother knelt at his feet. What was his pain as the nails were driven though his flesh? What were his thoughts as he allowed himself to be crucified? What manner of man was this who could suffer his life for all who had gone before or who would come after?"

"But in his face we saw only peace and a gentle innocence. His was a calmness born of great suffering but of even greater joy. I know we all felt the sweetness of his childlike spirit. Many in the throng that had gathered were now kneeling in worship, their hands together in prayers of gratitude. The Spirit made it known to me in that moment that all who saw him were in perfect accord regarding their love and loyalty to this man who is our Savior and Redeemer, who will be our Judge and Advocate with God the Father. My own eyes became wet as I beheld him. I longed to have him look at me, but he had come to bless my cousins, and his eyes were shut in prayer. We all did likewise, praying with him as he petitioned Father in Heaven on behalf of those two souls."

"'I am Jesus Christ. I am Jehovah, he who has taken upon himself the sins of worlds without number that all who repent with faith and come unto me may be saved in the halls of my holy Father, Creator of the universes and all that in them are. Father, I give all allegiance to Thee who dwellest in Thy heavens with Thy holy angels. Praised be Thy holy name.'"

"As his inspired words continued and he welcomed the Holy Ghost to dwell with the hearts of these spirits, I felt the impression that I should open my eyes. As I did so, I beheld a marvelous manifestation. A white dove had entered the room, coming to rest on a pillar nearby. It, too, gave off a bright and beautiful glow that radiated upon us. It appeared to devote its attention to the proceedings. I don't think anyone else saw the dove, because as I looked around I saw their eyes were shut, but the impression of the Holy Ghost was given to each of us, I am sure. How fortunate I was to see and hear these marvelous things!"

"The Savior continued to bless the children who knelt before him, in words of such spiritual beauty I cannot recall them. Surely only heaven itself could contain such holy testament."

The Lord finished his blessing and rose. He hugged each member of the family and spoke with them. Then he turned and looked directly at me. I felt the warmth of his penetrating glance. Quickly I turned to see his outstretched arms beckoning me. 'Come to me, my little one,' he said to my heart and to my spirit so hungry for his love. There were tears upon his face. I believe that I moved toward him, longing for his embrace, but suddenly the connection was broken and all I recall is the sun's insistent heat shining rudely in my face while I lay lost in joy upon my flannel pillow, far from the dulling territories of earth.

Sixteen

Marshall put his journal down. His tiredness overcame him. Ruth knew they'd have to stop now. She turned around to find Mrs. Willow listening to him, just inside the door. Now she moved to his bedside and the man smiled up at her.

"Grace, here, used to be a nurse among the Inuit up the Yukon way years ago. Now she's stuck with me," Marshall said fondly while she took his temperature. Her eyes avoided his.

"Now, Marshall Cannon, you rest. This story can wait until you've had your nap or you'll find yourself back in the hospital again." She shakes a pudgy finger at him, but he turns to me with raised eyebrows and a wink.

"We still have work to do here, Grace. Just give me a little while longer and I'll stop for the day, promise. Bring me some more water, will you, dear?"

Mrs. Willow grudgingly took the empty glass from Marshall's shaky hand. She pretended to consult her watch.

"You can have some time after dinner. I want you to rest, now. Please, Marshall. You need all your strength for this."

She and Ruth left the room to get the dinner trays and they all ate silently, thinking of the preparations that would inevitably have to be made, but Marshall was the only one who smiled.

It came to her on the beach beneath the madronas, where she had come after dinner while Marshall napped and Mrs. Willow made sure he had everything he would need near the bed. It was just a flurry at first, a rushing sound, like a swoosh that passed her ears and then turned and came back around. Ruth had been thinking about Marshall and his dreams, how his story would end. How much longer could he go on? Clearly, his energy was evaporating and his body longed for rest, but still he had more to tell. And Ruth longed to hear it, all that he had to tell, for it was changing her life as it had molded his. She was thinking about that when the sound came. First it filled her ears like a far off song, faint but with definite melody, like a radio in another room, and she wanted to find the source so she could turn up the volume. But the beach was empty and the house behind her shut to the water and wind of the bay.

Then she heard the words distinctly, apart from song. They came first to her heart, but somehow she was given to understand they were for her alone. They were beautiful words, almost a prayer, and Ruth realized she had almost despaired of ever hearing them. Grateful tears flowed from her now, and surprise and joy. She sat on the beach a long time feeling the miracle of it, until Mrs. Willow called her inside.

Marshall seemed stronger after his nap that had only lasted an hour. He greeted her gaily from beneath his oxygen mask and she had to laugh. Ruth was dear to him, steadfast. He would miss her loyalty, her willingness to record his most precious memories that his family could share its message. He wished they could have met years earlier and become fast friends.

Ruth looked at her dear friend. She couldn't imagine life without him any more. His happy spirit and his tenacity were a beacon in her life. She longed to tell him of her experience on the beach, but he was already opening his journal expectantly.

"Ahoy, matey. Hoist the sails again. Ready for another trip, are ye?"

"I'm ready, Marshall. Where is our trip taking us this time?"

Marshall laughed with the right side of his mouth.

"Let's go to an island, and let's finish the journey this trip, okay?"

"Finish the journey?" Ruth felt a chill beginning at the nape of her neck. "Do you mean you're almost through with the story?"

"Very soon, now, I'll be done, and we can wind this up. How about that?"

"Well," Ruth said, and her voice trailed away. Marshall saw her face. He reached out his hand to her and she took it.

"Don't you despair of me," he said. "You know, when our work is finished on this earth, the Lord takes us home and gives us more to do!"

"I know. But I'm not ready to lose you, yet. Maybe another twenty years or so."

Marshall laughed again, but it erupted in painful coughs. After a minute he said

"What about all those dates I have to keep in Heaven? If I'm late, they'll start without me. Better turn on that recorder so we can get started, don't you think?" He hoped that would help, but then he felt bad for teasing her.

"Now where did I leave off? After that vision of the Savior blessing that family, I was a changed person. I just awoke a different boy, a captivated spirit. I finally understood that the angels had taught me the truth. How can I tell you about what happened next? I awoke with a feeling of peace and harmony. The urge to run away was gone, but a new feeling came over me. It was a sense of freedom, of my own personality expanding and asserting itself in the world. I felt so happy. Now I needed to share it with the world, with the mountains and the sea, to sing to God as I rowed upon the waters of the peaceful bay in that glorious first morning of my new life. Just for awhile I had to commune, to be alone with God in that way. I needed time to rethink everything that had happened."

"As soon as I woke I dressed, grabbed my old pocket compass and went out. I headed toward the forest cove where I knew the canoe would be waiting, hidden in the trees. I was shaking with excitement. The boat was in its usual place, filled with leaves and other debris. A squirrel hopped out of it and rushed up a tree. I knew the boat shouldn't be taken out alone but today was special. All I could hear in my mind was the sound of that marvelous voice blessing that family. Even deeper than that, I remembered the look in the eyes of Christ."

"The bay was calm and flowing. The sun hid behind clouds that were high and streaming overhead. Far to the north there were darker masses, but I couldn't smell rain in the air. The wind was mild and the birds sang their praises to God. It was a good day to sail. I hurriedly cleared out the boat and inspected the oars. Old, dry and rotting, they would not stand much more than another winter without needing replacing, but I was just going to sail out to the little uninhabited island where with my buddies I

113

often played at being shipwrecked. I noticed an old coil of rope was still there to moor the boat. A rusty iron stake we had found some years past was still there, so we had sort of an anchor when we got to shore."

"The canoe had no tie line. All I had to do was shove it down the shore to the water, which I did with little trouble. The old crate squeaked over the stones, rumbling down the bank, taking me with it. One oar caught beneath the keel, so I had to flip the heavy old thing on its side to free it. Within a few minutes the canoe slid into the water with me jumping in it. Oh, the exhilarating feeling it gave me to be in that little boat! I sat on the thwart, grabbed the oars and set them in their locks, then I turned the canoe and navigated into the Sound, anxious to reach Lake Island three miles away. All the while I was thinking of my old pal Spank and the others and how they'd be hopping angry with me if they knew I was alone in our boat."

"At that low point in the shoreline the currents are shallow, but in the midst of the Sound land sinks to more than six fathoms. At that depth heavy currents unshackle the waves and they can be wild, unpredictable creatures. Suddenly, the left oar shaft split in two when I put effort against its roll. It rolled away, leaving a nasty cut in my hand. I should have turned toward home because I sensed the boat was not completely seaworthy, but I was foolish. While I rowed I remembered with regret that in all my years near the bay and the fishing boats I had never taken the time or effort to learn to swim well. That's when the idea of prayer first entered my heart, I think, to take time for praying to Heavenly Father for deliverance from that damned storm!"

But it was not yet to come. I had more turmoil to go through. Getting around the currents near the shoreline took some expert rowing and I was grateful that I knew something about navigation, simple as it was. Then, when I'd rowed about a mile, that weak oar broke in my hand on a pull-through stroke and before I could catch it a good part of the shaft and paddle were swept away!

"Now I was really in trouble. I only had one oar and the bow of the boat pointed north, despite my efforts. The wind pushed it into mid channel, where it bobbed crazily. Even with one oar I could do little but be tossed around. Water sloshed at my feet. My shivering increased until my whole body was in pain. Perhaps to help myself think I reached in my pocket and wrestled out my compass. The needle confirmed the northward heading but I could barely navigate in the wind and rain. The compass had proved useless, as the angels had predicted. Thunder banged against my eardrums. "Bear away before the wind" I shouted to an imaginary mate, and then I pulled and pushed that oar to right myself back to a northwest point on the port bow, but the bay's wildness overcame me at every stroke until I learned forever what it's like to be at the mercy of nature."

"The storm was worsening. The boat bobbed up and down like a rocking horse toy. I knew I couldn't even be seen from the main shoreline, and with one oar I might not reach it until I'd drifted many miles to the north, if I was lucky. My stomach churned with every lift and snap of the waves! I was so afraid I didn't know what to do.

"Then all at once it came to me. 'Pray,' the message clearly said. 'Get on your knees and pray for help.'"

And that's just what I did. I knelt, holding on to the sides of the boat, my eyes closed and the rain coming down in torrents on my bowed head. I prayed to God that He would save me. I shouted it out so He would hear. I told Him how sorry I was for messing up my life and for not believing in His words. I thanked Him for His angels and for my dreams. I told him my faith had grown and I begged for deliverance from the storm. I told Him I was afraid, that I didn't want to die. I told him I would dedicate my life to serving Him if He would get me out of this mess. I said a lot more and cried like a scared baby. Then - wait! How sudden it all came to me - this was a test! Just as Abraham was tested, and Alma! What did I need to know to pass, to survive this? Then, as surely as if I had always known, I said to the wind:

'Jesus is the Christ. I know the angels spoke the truth.'

The love of God had brought me here to be tested as I, the rebel, had tested Him. Where had that knowledge been hiding? Suddenly I just simply knew that my church was God's own, and it filled my whole being with tremors not of cold but of joy. New tears came to me as the rain washed them away. Now the storm became a celebration of faith in that rickety old boat. But I still had to get to shore. I started to row again, but I couldn't find the other oar. No iron rod, it had fallen out of its brace and was gone. I remember screaming in anger. I was at the mercy of the storm, no oars, no cover, no help in sight. You never realize how little separates man from the elements until certain death is a wave away. Only the thin staves of birchwood bargained my life from that cold, ruthless sea and I was very grateful for that tree!

"Let me tell you, my dear, what separates us from the love and mercy of God is the thinly veiled dimension we call this world, with it's faithless works, it's blind alleys and its devilish ways. That boat was my escape or my doom, it was transportation to safety or death upon the water, whatever choice I made there would follow me through life. So on my knees again in the watery bottom of that old boat I prayed all over again. Just me and God out there, one on one."

'Come and get me, Lord,' I said. 'Kill me or take me. Whatever your choice, I will be yours forever, and that is a solemn promise!'

"I looked up from my prayer. Fog had come in around me and I was losing my bearings fast. My compass lay in the watery bottom of the boat. It might as well have been at the bottom of the sea. I felt I was drowning. "And then I saw them, there on the shore, I think, but no, I couldn't see the shore. They must have been standing on the water, the two of them, in shirt and pants, real people there ahead of me, not a dream, but really here. I swear to you, I saw them in front of me, there on the water, in the fog."

Marshall was exhausted. He laid back, his eyes shut, the journal failing from him.

"Who was there, Marshall? Who did you see?"

Ruth heard him moan in pain. He's having another attack, he thought wildly and then yelled "Help!" and ran to get Mrs. Willow. They called the ambulance and it came in five more minutes. The women followed in Ruth's car. All the way to the hospital and throughout the night's urgent details, one question would not leave her alone. *How did you make it to shore?*

116

Seventeen

Somewhere in the night they were offered an empty hospital room down the hall from Marshall's. Ruth, always a good sleeper, fell into dreams right away. It wasn't yet dawn when she felt the weighty hand of Mrs. Willow.

"Sit up," she said, tears choking her. "Come down to his room with me."

As Ruth sat up, she knew. Her dream vanished.

"What's happened?"

"He's going, they said, his doctors. They said he's going fast."

She was crying and wiping her nose at the same time. Ruth had fallen asleep dressed. Together they ran to Marshall's room. Marshall lay in low light, so still in that impersonal metal-railed bed, an attitude of attention upon his features. His nurse hurried past us as we entered, but the look on her face said it all. He hadn't stayed for goodbyes, at the last. Had Silas and Barak come to take him home? Ruth imagined him hurrying to Naida's waiting arms. She thought he must have carried that same look of intense wonder and concentration on his face as he sailed in his dreams to distant lands with the voices of angels in his ears. His death in this life would be cause for celebration in the next.

Ruth sank into a chair and let the pain of loss overwhelm her. For a long time she was drained of energy, caught up in her grief. Well, she thought, we almost made it. You were a brave man, you ran a good race. The tears I shed for you, my friend, are tears of being left behind. Mrs. Willow, his faithful cousin, took Marshall's lifeless hands in hers. Her usually efficient and pragmatic demeanor was gone. Love for her cousin overcame her and she sobbed, failing across his bed.

"Marsh," she whispered. "Oh, Marsh, thank you for all those years. What would I have ever done without you?"

She lay there a long time with him. But Marshall had left them his mystery. Ruth would have to finish the task for him, he wanted that, she was sure. Her mind kept going over all the possibilities of their last moments together, but nothing helped her to finish the story. How could she speculate a miracle? *How had he reached the shore?*

Marshall Cannon's funeral was large and well attended. A gregarious man, he kept in touch with hundreds of friends as Ruth discovered watching Mrs. Willow diligently making the fateful calls from her "place" in the kitchen. In the interim between her cousin's death and internment she refused to approach his office, but shut it up as if it were a shrine, changing and remaking his bed, then waxing and dusting the room's furniture. Then she decided to clean the whole house in between crying sessions on the outside davenport. Ruth tried to console her and made her own tired way home to change and pack for the return trip. At Mrs. Willow's very tearful request she'd agreed to help with final plans.

The condolences were an avalanche. They came from everywhere, it seemed to her, to pay their respects to this man whose life and spiritual energy had in some way lent inspiration to their own. Ruth was quickly drawn into the homes and hearts of Marshall's family and friends, many of whom were not members of the Church. Many were the moving testimonies of "Marsh," his caring and frequent gifts of money and other needed things to those who he watched over from afar. He had been to many souls an untiring missionary for Christ, giving away hundreds of Book of Mormons, bibles, and the like. They reminisced of his kindness and generosity and mourned him. Their love was his epitaph.

But his story was incomplete. Marshall had died before he divulged the ending. Ruth worried about turning over the tapes and notes as they were. If she could just get into his locked study, surely the journal would have the last entries. Following the funeral she sat in the large living room with Mrs. Willow, listening to stories of her years spent with Marshall. A longtime widow and lonely, Grace had come to call on Marshall one day in the fog of time past. He had understood her loneliness; it was akin to his own. Eventually he asked her to stay, just simply like that, and she did so. Together they came to share a deep trust, attended by a shared passion for the sea. Their lively

118

conversations, which she seemed to remember word for word, were precious to her.

Ruth listened with sympathy for her loss. She wondered just how much Marshall had told her...

"Mrs. Willow, did Marshall ever share his dreams with you?"

Grace Willow looked away for a moment, as if protecting a confidence. Slowly she said

"Oh, yes, a little. Not much, but just something about those times when he was young and had those dreams."

She said "dreams" as if she also thought them odd.

With trepidation Ruth ventured further, telling the older woman about that last interview with Marshall. While she spoke Grace covered her face with her hands. Ruth didn't know if she should go on, but then Grace agreed to unlock his room and let Ruth see the journal.

"We didn't speak of it, he and I. But, yes, I'm sure that Marsh would want you to know more about those last minutes."

She smiled at Ruth with knowing in her eyes, and suddenly Ruth realized she knew. He had told her and she knew and now she would lead Ruth to the answer. How much more was there to tell? Grace stood and found her keys. Together the women walked down the hall to the study and whatever answers were waiting there. As the door opened the scene of Marshall in his chair, vibrant and purposeful, suddenly reappeared. Tears came to Ruth's eyes. Mrs. Willow gave a gasp and turned to her hurriedly.

"His journal's in there, I'm sure, as he left it. You're welcome to look for what you need. We'll need lunch. Let me know if I can help."

Sniffling, she moved with more than her customary hurry back to the kitchen. Ruth called out her gratitude but Mrs. Willow bobbed her head without turning around.

Now alone in his paper-strewn study, leftovers of a busy and fulfilling life, Ruth rummaged for the journal. It wasn't on the desk or in the drawers. Where had he put it? There were cabinets across the room, flanking a side wall. They were unlocked. She pulled them open one by one. The first was full of invoices relative to his business as a navigational engineer. The second contained articles pertaining to the Church: pamphlets, booklets, talks given and handouts galore, gathered for years, no doubt, in ready reference if needed. The third and bottom drawer was too heavy to open. Ruth imagined it contained a personal safe or other private records. A label on it said simply "Marshall". She knew his journal had to be within ready reach of him, so she resumed her search of his bookcase area.

A small old brown cardboard box next to his desk was partly open. A framed picture of a very young Marshall standing next to a slender, high-cheeked, dark-haired woman looked out at me, no doubt taken with his wife, Naida during their short life together. He was laughing, young, robust and happy. She peered up at him, love in her eyes. They looked wonderful together, she in her dress of animal pelts, he in a parka that looked too small for his large frame. Further search revealed letters addressed to Marshall from Naida and others. Ruth looked at the postmarked dates on the envelopes. Many were between forty and fifty years old, spanning the years between the time of his marriage to Naida and his final business endeavors. She did not breach the privacy of the lives in those letters, but dug deeper.

Her fingers touched something hard. It revealed a book, smelling of musty leather, its cover held by a small clasp into which was fit a leather tongue. It fit in her hand as she turned it over. It was dark and somewhat torn from handling. Curiosity overcame her. She unsnapped the top and opened the book.

The first notation was dated March 1. Scribbled in what she was coming to recognize as Marshall's handwriting were the words: *She is gone. My life's only true love is with our God. This day in gratitude to Him that my darling and I will one day be together again, I dedicate my mission.*

His mission? He had never told Ruth about a mission. The second entry revealed that he had been assigned to proselyte the seemingly limitless territory of vast northern Canada, then a primitive area. He told of the few supplies he carried, of meeting his companion, a Frenchman named Jacques Touville, from Winnipeg. They had to live in very difficult circumstances, sometimes out of tents, as they went among the Indian tribes teaching the Gospel of Jesus Christ to any who would listen, and many who did they baptized there in the freezing lakes and rivers of that rugged terrain. It went on in some detail for two years, ending with his tally of 12 women, 6 children, 24 men, all baptized, and his final words: *In the years 1938-40, following the death of my beloved, I have completed my mission for the Lord.*

So that's what happened to Marshall! After Naida's death he became a missionary for the Church. What a declaration of faith! She counted the number of converts who he led to the Lord, wondering how many others had stemmed from the original forty-two through the years. Closing the little journal like a precious jewel, Ruth returned it to the bottom of the box.

Finally, in a desk corner almost fallen against a pile of books on the sea, it's yellowed pages facing me, she found the old gray journal. Gingerly, aware now of its suddenly inestimable value, she opened it. There were small drawn pictures of angels in attitudes of prayer on the first page, and the words "My Adventures With the Angels of Love - PRIVATE" written in serious large letters below the pictures. It began with Marshall's story as he had told it to her, full of his discoveries, quotes from Barak and Silas, more quotes and citations from scripture, long, detailed descriptions of the upper and lower Sound, thoughts and memories of childhood. During our interviews Marshall had taken a lot verbatim from his journal so he would not have to rely only on memory for his amazing dream history. Ruth continued to turn the pages, following the story as he'd told it to her.

She'd almost finished the book when she reached the words "Father, unto Thee I give my life" and found the final episode of his tryst with the sea. Here was the story of his taking the boat and sailing to the island. The storm that came up was recorded in vivid detail, but she was surprised to find that it ended where their dictation had - with no mention of how he'd reached the western shore from the island. Marshall had hastily notated two citations on an otherwise blank page that referred to 1John 4:18 and Doctrine and Covenants 61:6. Why didn't he record this final, most important part? Ruth felt a sense of hopelessness, not knowing where else to look for the answer. She stared at the

121

scripture citation, then reached across the desk for the Bible, an old and much-thumbed black tome. Turning to 1John, she read,

There is no fear in love; but perfect love casteth out fear. Then she looked up Doctrine and Covenants 61:6 and read it. It referred to a situation in which the Prophet Joseph Smith and others in his party had concerns about their safety on the Missouri River in a canoe on a trip to Kirtland, Ohio in 1831:

Nevertheless, all flesh is in mine hand, and he that is faithful among you shall not perish by the waters.

Eighteen

Was the message in these scriptures? They were obviously set purposely upon the page following Marshall's sighting (or vision) of men (or angels) who appeared before him in the storm. Ruth turned the page, looking for more clues. On the otherwise empty page, at the bottom, easy to miss or mistake for childish doodling, she found a drawing of a canoe with lines beneath it to suggest a calm sea. A simply drawn figure of a boy stands in the canoe, leaning forward, arms outstretched, one foot on the bow. Across the page is a second figure draped in what appears to be a gown, with hair to his shoulders, arms beckoning. He leans forward toward the figure in the boat. Beneath it are the simple but profound words in quotes:

"Come to me, my son, and I will be with thee."

Ruth recalled suddenly Marshall's emphasizing that the sea can be tamed and that Jesus once walked upon it, urging Paul to step out of his fishing boat at sea to join his Savior. She let out a breath and leaned back, amazed at the implications. In her mind the young boy's triumphant act of faith was enacted and completed in the arms of a merciful Savior. Could such things happen in our time? Had there truly been a miracle there in the storm? She would never know just what happened upon the water, but in some miraculous way his life was saved and purchased and he dedicated the rest of his years to the Lord's work. Was this what he had kept from the world? Even here in his private journal he only partly disclosed those transforming moments when his trust was tried and made perfect.

Mrs. Willow entered the room at that precise moment, seeing the journal, and Ruth's face. She set the tea down and quietly sat near Ruth. Tears filled her eyes, as if this moment was the fulfillment of many years of unspoken testimony, held in a sacred trust.

"Ruth, Marsh used to say that when the student is ready, the teacher will appear." I think you're ready now."

She reached into the narrow pocket of her dress and extracted a small envelope of the sort that encloses a card or thank you note. Ruth's name was scrawled across it in Marshall's webby handwriting. It was sealed.

"Marshall wanted you to have this. He wrote it after one of your last interviews together. He said that you could understand it better than anyone... He said that *The Press On* is yours, too, if you want her."

Ruth took the envelope and let it lay in her lap. It seemed as if all of the time the three of them had spent together had come to this one moment. All that she was looking for waited there in that sealed blue envelope. The older woman stood to leave but Ruth moved to stop her.

"Do you know what's in here?" she asked her.

"No. It's yours alone, as Marshall wanted."

"What about that day on the water, Grace? Do you know who he saw there?"

Grace Willow bowed her head and a sweet smile came to her lips. When she looked up she was crying.

"Now I am free to tell you. He saw our Savior there, and walked to him from the boat."

Their eyes met and they sat there in the afternoon light, almost in tableau.

"He walked on the water? He told you that?"

"Yes. He said when he left the boat to join the angels and the Savior, he seemed to be dreaming that he was put ashore and when he looked down, he saw the sand was beneath him. The canoe was evidently lost in the storm, but he was safe. That's what he told me, and then he made me promise to tell no one else. I've kept it in here - she touched her chest - all these long years."

She breathed a grateful sigh of relief.

"It feels so good now, to share it with you."

Ruth let it sink in. That's why Marshall hadn't recorded the story, not even in his journal, for those of lesser faith to find. It was sacred to him, and like all sacred things, shared with great care.

Mrs. Willow's smile was kind.

"You are only the second person to know, but he will want his family to know, also. Will you put it in with his story?"

"Of course I will. I've been so desperate to know. Thank you, Grace, but what if I hadn't come along? He'd never have told them?"

"He knew you'd come. He was promised it and when little David talked about his English teacher, Marshall received revelation that you were the one he'd been waiting for."

Ruth was stunned.

"He knew? He was waiting for me? Oh, my gosh. I don't believe it, and I was so close to saying no and just forgetting it... What if I'd done that?"

But Mrs. Willow was silent and still but for the brushing away of tears. Ruth looked at the envelope that still lay in her lap. She turned it over slowly, then with a fingernail began to pry up the seal. Inside was a short note, again scribbled in a hasty hand, but with ran strokes. Ruth read it out loud.

I have saved this for the last. Love is the only miracle, isn't it, the first and the final mystery? When I saw my Savior waiting on the water, I was small in my understanding, a cold, wet cripple of a boy full of fear and near drowning. Then he called to me and I reached out to him. He was radiant in his white gown. The storm didn't approach him. His feet were not even touching the water but he seemed to be standing solidly on some other, firm plane. His face was beautiful and his eyes full of love.

"Come to me, my little one, " he said quietly. Though the storm was intense and cracking all around us, I heard him clearly and when he spoke it moved me without my even thinking, for he spoke to my heart and I had to go to him. I just walked out of the boat, longing to touch his robes. Somehow, I was already there, standing with him on the water."

"Savior, " I said, too awed for crying. "Oh, my Savior. "

He looked at me, then, but no, he looked into me, into my very self, and he examined each part and every thought I'd ever known, and his eyes were like beacons of light, searching me in my deepest parts. I could not move or take my eyes from him, and I thought death would take me at that moment in a burst of white fire. Then his features softened but his gaze never left me.

Marshall, my son, hast thou faith in thy Christ? Does thou love thy Savior?

"Yes, Father, I do love thee. I know now thou art my Christ."

And I felt it, Ruth, felt it a real thing springing from me, passionate, the truest thing I have ever known.

"Then, my precious son, be thou whole; for thou art forever mine."

And then, Ruth, I reached out to him and touched his white robe. As I felt it, his words wrote themselves forever upon and within me, like a blessing and then like a shield. I was covered with peace, filled with joy and wonder, glorious with the new gladness that I belonged to the very one who had created me, sealed with him in a perfect moment of our faith and love.

I had been a foolish child living for what pleasures the world offered. But this man came to me, the only Begotten Son of God, and fed me love and hope. **Love** *is the secret, Ruth.* **His love.** *I learned in an instant that healing comes* **only** *from* **his selfless embrace.**

Now you know my most precious secret. I give it to you and to my dear family. Tell it to them and keep it in your heart, will you?

Your eternal friend, Captain Marshall L. Cannon
In a year of our Lord

Nineteen

In the days that followed, with a joyous and grateful heart, Ruth helped her new friend pack food, then carried the suitcases and other belongings Grace would need for the trip down the coast to Ruth's home. The ocean, black at night, never sleeps but is sullen without the light of day. In the winning sky billions of luminous lights define the paths of galaxies and it is easy to imagine the white-clothed angels of God in careful charge of each returning spirit as it ascends toward Paradise. The women, their hearts full of new beginnings, marveled at the beauty of the evening along the Sound and talked about Ruth's plan to take a leave of absence from teaching.

In her heart was the legacy Marshall had left her, his inspired gift. And in her own new dreams she walked happily among the souls of a city with an eager companion. They carried well-thumbed Book of Mormons in their backpacks and prayers of living gratitude in their hearts.

Sometimes, at the close of her busy day, Ruth would reach into her heavy backpack and withdraw the little wooden replica of a single masted boat, its sail furled. She'd imagine Marshall there, talking with Silas and Barak, learning the wondrous truths she was now teaching others.

"What is that little boat?" her companions would ask Ruth.

"It's called *The Press On*", Ruth would begin, those simple words calling up precious memories. "I inherited it from one of the Lord's finest servants. Would you like to hear the story?"

The End

127

It is very important that we do not assume the perspective of mortality in making decisions that bear on eternity.

Elder Neal A. Maxwell
Quorum of the Twelve Apostles
1974

A Scriptural Index

By Chapter and Verse

Part One: Chapter One

The Essential Brigham Young
Signature Books, Salt Lake City
1992   page 35

Part Two: Chapter Five

There is none else save God that knowest thy thoughts and the intents of thy heart.
Doctrine and Covenants 6:16

Chapter Six

But when they in their trouble did turn unto the Lord God of Israel, and sought him, he was found of them.
2Chronicles 15:4

My son, if thou wilt receive my words, and hide my commandments with thee; so that thou incline thine ear to wisdom, and apply thine heart to understanding.
Proverbs 2:1-2

Trust in the Lord with all thine heart; and lean not unto thine own understanding. In all thy ways acknowledge him, and he shall direct thy paths...My son, despise not the chastening of the LORD, neither be weary of his correction.
Proverbs 3:5,6,11

Chapter Seven

...they who have faith in him will cleave unto every good thing; wherefore he advocateth every good thing;...and because he hath done this, my beloved brethren, have miracles ceased? Behold I say unto you, Nay; neither have angels ceased to minister unto the children of men. For behold, they are subject unto him...
    Moroni 7:28-30

Chapter Eight

For God, who commanded the light to shine out of darkness, hath shined in our hearts, to give the light of the knowledge of the glory of God in the face of Jesus Christ.
    2Corinthians 4:6

Part Three: Chapter Nine

I wander through the still of night...
Excerpt from *Come Unto Him*. Text by Theodore E. Curtis and music by Hugh W. Dougal
Hymns of the Church of Jesus Christ of Latter-day Saints,
The Church of Jesus Christ of Latter-day Saints, Salt Lake City 1985. Page 114

Part Four: Chapter 11

I say unto you, can ye look up to God at that day with a pure heart and clean hands? I say unto you, can you look up, having the image of God engraven upon your countenances?
    Alma 5:19

Chapter Eleven

And I, God, made two great lights; the greater light to rule the day, and the lesser light to rule the night, and the greater light was the sun, and the lesser light was the moon, and the stars also were made even according to my word.. And I, God, set them in the firmament of the heaven to give light upon the earth.
Moses 2:16-17, Pearl of Great Price

In the beginning God created the heaven and the earth... The light which is in all things, which giveth life to all things, which is the law by which all things are governed, even the power of God who sitteth upon his throne, who is in the bosom of eternity, who is in the midst of all things... And again, verily I say unto you, he hath given a law unto all things, by which they move in their times and their seasons; and their courses are fixed, even the courses of the heavens and the earth, which comprehend the earth and all the planets
Doctrine and Covenants 88:1; 42-43

Chapter Twelve

...have ye spiritually been born of God? Have ye received his image in your countenances? Have ye experienced this mighty change in your hearts?
Alma 5:14

Wherefore I give unto them a commandment... Thou shalt love the Lord thy God with all thy heart, with all thy might, mind and strength; and in the name of Jesus Christ thou shalt serve him. Thou shalt love thy neighbor as thyself...
Doctrine and Covenants 59:5-6

Author's Notes:

For those readers who are not familiar with the *Book of Mormon*, the names Alma, Zeezrom, Nephi and others, are early prophets in that true record of civilization on the North and South American continents from the time 600 b.c. until a.d. 421..

The *Doctrine and Covenants* is an inspired gathering of revelations from the Savior to his latter -day prophets regarding the restoration of his church upon the earth.

The Pearl of Great Price is also latter-day scripture discovered and purchased by the Prophet Joseph Smith and contains revelatory and insightful material about many bible subjects including premortal and postmortal existence.

Prophet Brigham Young was successor to the first latter-day prophet, Joseph Smith, who translated the Book of Mormon, a holy work and a companion to the Bible.

The church referred to in this book is *The Church of Jesus Christ of Latter-day Saints.*

About the Author

Marlena Tanya Muchnick is a longtime resident of the Pacific Northwest, the setting for this novel. Marlena writes as an inspired avocation. She is currently finishing *Songs in the Spirit*, a collection of inspirational stories, poems and essays. A children's book, *Anythingspossible Penguin,* is also in the works. Miss Muchnick invites all who are moved by her stories to communicate with her through her email address at myambra@hotmail.com or to log onto http://jewishconvert-lds.com for updates on talks, books signings and information on Judaica.

About the Illustrator

Denise A. Parrish makes her first foray into the world of professional illustration with her cover art and sketches for this book. She has had no formal training. Denise, an avid gardener, novice woodcarver and beaded jewelry artist, is a lifetime resident of the Pacific Northwest. She plans to visit the Holy Land with her sketchbook in the near future.